JONNY JAKES

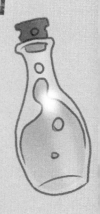

THE OLD SCHOOL GHOUL

Malcolm Judge

Curious
Fox

To Dom

Tuesday 8th January

National Bubble Bath Day

I'll accidentally mention it really loudly outside the geography office.

I'm Jonny Jakes.

If you think I'm telling you my real name, think again.

I'm an undercover reporter for *The Woodford Word*. It's the unofficial newspaper for Woodford School.

Last term I saved the world from being eaten by a family of bloodthirsty aliens. Today I got set three lots of homework and had cauliflower cheese for lunch.

Apparently life isn't fair.

On the plus side, we sold a lot of newspapers. Julie Singh reckons we sold over one hundred thousand copies.

That's a lot of 50ps.

We had a meeting at the end of last term to decide what to do with the money. I said that as Editor and Chief Executive of *The Woodford Word* I should have most of the money so I can invest it in the paper's future. Julie reckoned it was only fair to share the money equally between all of us.

She's like that.

Sally Coyle got out her calculator and pushed a few buttons. She said that, using a formula which accounted for how long each of us had worked on the paper, as well as factoring in the seniority of my position, her calculations suggested I was eligible to receive 56.34% of the profit margin.

Norris told her to speak properly.

I asked Sally if we were talking about a jar-full of cash or a bucket-full.

She said I'd probably have enough money to fill up a medium-sized suitcase.

I agreed that it seemed a very good formula.

As soon as I got home with the money, I went to work on a new disguise. I needed to look like a flashy businessman. I had the false moustache, I had the mirrored sunglasses, and I had a slightly smaller version of my dad's old wedding suit that mysteriously went missing from his wardrobe last summer.

Most importantly, I had a suitcase full of cash.

I wheeled the suitcase into town, doing my best to look cool. It's not easy when you're pulling half a ton of fifty pence pieces behind you. Once I'd got my breath back,

I went into the massive computer store and snapped my fingers at the nearest shop assistant. He didn't look very pleased about it, but I had a character to keep up.

I asked him for three new laptops, a top-of-the-range telescopic camera and an industrial-sized photocopier. I wanted them brought round when I knew my parents would be out visiting my granny. I took off my shades, gave him a wink and told him I'd make it worth his while if he could get them all delivered to my house in a white, unmarked van at 2.30 p.m. on Sunday, no questions asked.

He said he was going to call the police.

Then I opened my suitcase.

I could get used to being rich.

It's not easy being famous and trying to keep your true identity a secret. Thanks to *The Woodford Word*, everybody knows that I saved the world by defeating Mr Jones and his evil horde of flesh-eating children.

However, no one knows what I look like, because they

JONNY JAKES SAVES THE WORLD

Not content with defending truth and justice, undercover schoolboy reporter Jonny Jakes has now saved the world

were all in a weird hamburger-induced daze at the time. All sorts of dodgy people are offering a reward for information that might lead to the discovery of my real name.

Luckily, no one thinks an eleven-year-old is capable of award-winning journalism.

Norris can't understand why I don't just come forward and get all the glory. He says I could get myself on one of those television shows where celebrities get to mess about and make fools of themselves in front of millions of viewers.

I told him it was embarrassing enough walking through the middle of Woodford every day wearing a school uniform that's exactly the same colour as sick.

Maybe I'll think about it when my skin stops exploding into spots at the sight of chips. Or when I feel the need to impress girls.

Mum keeps reminding me that's about to happen any time now.

Speaking of girls, there's one in particular I'm trying to avoid. Michelle Bell.

Every time I see her I have to dive for cover. She doesn't know I'm Jonny Jakes, but she does know I've got something to do with *The Woodford Word*. She found me and Norris intercepting letters from our old head teacher, Mr Hardy, last term and threatened to tell if she didn't get her own fashion page in the paper. I'm hoping that, because *The Woodford Word* helped save her from aliens, she'll keep her mouth shut.

Unfortunately that doesn't happen very often.

Unbelievable! Karl Huck is going to pretend to be me. Julie heard it in the dinner queue.

Karl Huck has more stupid ideas than actual brain cells to have them with. At Christmas he swapped the fairy on top of the school's Christmas tree with a pair of his underpants. He thought it would be funny. Everyone else just wished he'd remembered to wash them first.

Being Karl Huck, he hadn't realized that his mum had sewn a name tag into them. He got suspended for a week.

It made a great front page for the festive issue of *The Woodford Word*, though:

THE WOODFORD WORD

UNLUCKY HUCKY

Karl Huck decided to add his own decoration to the school Christmas tree this week: his pants. Unluckily for him, his mum wasn't so keen on him leaving them lying around.

I guess he wants to get his own back.

Norris volunteered to get hold of Karl's memory stick. If he's put any fake *Woodford Word* material on it, we can use it to expose him. Julie said she'd mention Karl's name at home to see if it got any reaction from her mum. Julie's mum, Mrs Singh, is the Head's secretary and talks loudly about everything.

That's the main reason I let Julie work for the paper.

Sally said she'd ask her friends to see if she could get anything useful. I said I didn't think she had any friends. She said she knows Andrea Mollov from swimming club, who is best friends with Molly Shearer who used to walk in to school with someone who lived across the road from Karl Huck.

I won't hold my breath.

If I can get enough material together for a paper, at least the headline won't be difficult:

HUCK SUCKS

Time to get to work.

Thursday 10th January

Another year and already another triumph for *The Woodford Word*. We managed to get the paper out this morning and Karl Huck is now officially the least popular boy in school.

Or he would be if he wasn't at home pretending to be ill.

Just because Norris Morris is really big, has a stupid name and smiles a lot, everyone thinks he's stupid. People underestimate him. That's why Norris managed to get Karl Huck out of the computer room yesterday. He told him he'd been ordered to go over to Mr Hamed's office to pick up a long weight.

He'd still be waiting now if the cleaner hadn't explained.

Norris found Karl's so-called newspaper on the memory stick he left behind. Karl had used all his brainpower to encrypt it in a file named 'DROWDROFDOOWEHT'.

Karl Huck wouldn't know what cunning was if it jumped out in front of him in bright yellow boxing gloves and broke his nose.

According to him, good headlines to use would have been:

WE'RE TIE-ERED OF TIES

for an article complaining about Sixth Formers having to wear uniform;

LOOPY SOUPY MACHINE

for a story complaining about how the drinks machine keeps breaking; and

PICS AND KICKS

about how the Year Ten football team got their picture in the local paper before their third round County Cup match.

I've never been so insulted in my life.

As well as exposing Karl's plan to try and fool everyone,

we blew up a picture Sally had found of him when he was a toddler. It's brilliant. He's sitting at a table concentrating on trying to do some drawing with a really big pen. But there's nothing on the paper in front of him and he's looking really frustrated.

That's because he's holding the pen the wrong way round.

HUCK SUCKS!

In a clumsy attempt to impersonate *The Woodford Word's* star reporter, Karl Huck has once again come off second best.

I think Sally's starting to get the hang of the newspaper business.

I've still got one resolution left.
That's a new record.

Michelle Bell was lying in wait for me today.

She was hiding behind the penguin sculpture as I came out of the library at break. Just because I've got something to do with a newspaper she thinks I'm a nerd.

'I want a word with you, nerd!' she sneered, grabbing my tie and pinning me against the wall.

'Go for it,' I wheezed, trying to sound casual despite the lack of oxygen reaching my brain.

'You've been avoiding me,' she hissed, covering me in spit.

'Sorry. It's just my mum told me to keep away from people who try to strangle me.'

'And I will if you don't shut up and listen,' she spat again, giving me an extra shove against the wall.

I decided to shut up and listen.

'That paper you work for hasn't been very nice about my boyfriend!'

'But ... we...' I attempted to protest. 'We hadn't written anything about Trevor Neave.'

'My *new* boyfriend,' Michelle clarified. 'And I don't like it when people are nasty about my boyfriends. So, you tell them that I want to know who Jonny Jakes is or I'm going to see what happens when I pull this even tighter.'

She pulled the knot on my tie hard up against my neck and then suddenly released me. She marched off as I crumpled against the penguin and scratched my face on one of the flippers.

I hate that stupid penguin.

I told Norris how we were going to deal with the Michelle Bell situation.

He said he didn't hit girls.

He said he knew Michelle Bell was going out with Karl Huck. I asked him why. He said it paid to keep up with other people's love lives because you never knew when the information might come in useful.

I don't know how Michelle Bell keeps up with her own love life.

I called an emergency board meeting at the picnic table next to the wildlife garden. One day *The Woodford Word* will get the office space it truly deserves.

'So, what are we going to do about her?' I asked. 'If she opens her mouth it's going to be a disaster.'

'We'd still carry on the paper without you,' Sally piped up enthusiastically.

'You see what I mean!' I yelled, banging my fist on the table.

'Oi! We're quite capable of doing things without you, thank you very much,' Julie complained.

'Oh, sure you are! Just like you came up with something on Karl Huck when it really mattered.'

Julie went a little red in the face. 'Actually, I did have something, but...'

'But what?' I demanded. 'He was about to ruin our reputation!'

'But I wasn't sure you'd handle it in a sensitive manner,' Julie said quietly. 'In fact, I'm not sure you're capable of handling anything in a sensitive manner.'

Julie had gone really red in the face now. I thought about shouting 'BEEEETROOOOT' but I had a feeling it might have proved her point.

Julie took a deep breath and continued.

'It's just, I'm not sure I want to be part of a newspaper that's always pointing out all the bad things about the school. I mean, would it kill us just to be positive for a change?'

I couldn't believe what I was hearing.

'What about our coverage on the Under Twelves' hockey team winning the District Cup final against West Shire School?' I pointed out. 'Surely that was a positive story?'

'That wasn't positive,' Julie moaned. 'The headline was HOW DIRE ARE SHIRE?'

'Some of them couldn't even hold their sticks the right way round!'

'That's not the point!'

'Yes it is!' I insisted. 'We only beat them because their own defender forgot which way she was meant to hit the puck and scored an own goal!' I was getting pretty red in the face myself now. 'There is such a thing as the truth, you know, or can't you handle it? And the truth is we only won that match because the other team were even worse than we were!'

Me and Julie were face to face now and breathing heavily. You could have cut the air with a breadstick.

Sally coughed. 'Actually, it's a ball.'

'What?!' me and Julie shouted, still glaring at each other.

'It's only called a puck in ice-hockey,' Sally whispered.

If Sally had been trying to clear the air, it hadn't worked. Julie gave me one last glare, then turned on her heel and left. Sally hesitated and then ran after her.

I asked Norris if he was absolutely sure he didn't hit girls.

I've spent the weekend wondering how to deal with Michelle Bell. If she starts using my name in connection with *The Woodford Word* my Jonny Jakes days are over.

I needed to cheer myself up so I Googled myself again and surfed through the millions of articles and pictures about my famous victory over Mr Jones. You could actually see me in some of them, but without a big arrow pointing it out, no one would ever know who I really was.

And all it took to change that was Michelle Bell and her massive gob.

I decided to check the pictures for ones of her. To throw darts at them.

That's when I found it. I was looking through an online Japanese newspaper site. The Japanese love me. There was a picture of a busy school corridor. It was the day the school re-opened. Everyone's still looking a bit shell-shocked. And there, standing near the bottom of the stairs, was Michelle Bell.

It wasn't just the gormless look on her face. It wasn't the extra padding on her bottom after being fed a diet of mega-fattening hamburgers. Everyone still had that. It was the fact she'd forgotten to straighten her hair.

And when Michelle Bell forgets to straighten her hair, she looks like an electrocuted poodle.

Monday 14th January

This time it was my turn to lie in wait for Michelle Bell. I hid behind the wheelie bins at break and waited for her to reapply her make-up. It didn't take long.

'Remember me?' I said, reaching into my pocket and holding up a copy of her picture between my fingers. 'You know, the one you tried to strangle behind the penguin?'

Michelle Bell looked confused, so I pressed home my advantage.

'It's not very nice being threatened, is it?'

I'd hoped for some sort of reaction, but Michelle Bell didn't seem to be bothered. She pulled an eyeliner pencil out of her make-up bag and pointed it at my upraised hand.

'Why are you waving a sweet wrapper at me, you moron?'

I cursed my stupidity and reached back in my pocket for the picture.

'What's that supposed to be?' Michelle demanded when I finally managed to pull out the crumpled bit of paper.

'It's a picture. Of you.'

'So what?' Michelle grunted, unimpressed.

'Take a closer look,' I said and tossed the picture towards her.

It would have been cooler if it hadn't fallen right into a puddle.

I picked the picture out of the puddle, wiped it and passed it over. Michelle Bell brought it slowly to her face. Her eyes widened and she let out a tiny gasp.

At last I had her at my mercy.

Her fingers were up my nostrils so quickly I didn't even have time to blink. Michelle Bell put the picture right in front of my watering eyes.

'If anyone else sees this I'll rip your nose clean off your face.'

I tried to say 'If you kill me we will publish this picture every day for a month,' but I think it just sounded like, 'AAHHHHHHHHHHHHHHHHHHHHHHHHHHHHHH!'

'What!?'

It was pointless trying to talk with silver glitter fingers up my nose. It was hard enough trying to breathe. I pulled out the piece of paper Norris had made me carry in my pocket. He'd warned me that this sort of thing might happen.

'*If I get hurt we will publish this picture every day for a month,*' Michelle Bell read. She thought about it, then reluctantly let me go.

'You know, one day I'm going to find out who that Jonny Jakes is. And when I do, I'm gonna...'

She didn't finish her sentence. Imagination isn't Michelle Bell's strong point.

'Get lost!' she snarled, ripping up the picture and tossing it in the nearest bin.

It wasn't going to be easy in the school playground, but I gave it a go.

After lunch we had assembly. We used to have them in the morning, but it's part of Mr Chattersly's new routine, along with compulsory water bottles and letting the Sixth Formers call him Alistair.

Mr Chattersly is the Acting Head Teacher.

That means he isn't a proper one, but it hasn't stopped him changing everything.

'Now then, everybody,' Mr Chattersly began. 'Let's just pause to reflect for a moment, shall we?'

Mr Chattersly paused for reflection and swept back his wavy brown hair with his fingertips. I'm pretty sure the main reason Mr Chattersly pauses to reflect is just so that he can sweep back his wavy brown hair with his fingertips.

'It strikes me,' Mr Chattersly continued, 'that we live in a time that values cynicism over positivity. A time that encourages putting something down, rather than building something up. A time, if you like, that prefers sneering over cheering.'

Mr Chattersly thinks he has a way with words. That's why he uses so many of them.

'Now, I want to change all that. You all know I'm a history teacher, so you won't be surprised that I think we can learn an awful lot from studying the past.

'Not so long ago this country was very proud of itself, and for good reason! We used to lead the world in innovation and technology. Our inventors, explorers and craftsmen were the envy of the world. Ask a Victorian gentleman what he thought of his country and he'd tell you it was the home of all that was great and good.

'So, I was thinking, why don't we try and be a little more like the Victorians? I don't mean let's all have massive sideburns and wear top hats,' Mr Chattersly left a brief pause so that everyone could laugh.

When nobody did, he turned it into a longer pause and tried to make it look like that's what he meant to do in the first place. Then he added some pacing up and down a bit, and wagging a finger at nothing in particular.

'I mean, of course,' he said, struggling to get back into his rhythm, 'let's try and think a little more like the Victorians, shall we? Rather than think the worst of ourselves, why don't we try celebrating our good side? Let's not be afraid of singing our own praises! Let's not be afraid of banging our own drum! And, most of all, let's not be afraid of blowing our own trumpet.'

Mr Chattersly thumped his fist on the lectern. He was pumped up again now.

'And so, to encourage a new spirit of optimism and pride amongst you, I am hereby launching a competition to create a new, official school newspaper. Yes! You heard me!' Mr Chattersly cried triumphantly, as his audience slowly came back to life and Matthew Roberts stopped trying to flick my ears.

'We thank Jonny Jakes for what he did last term, but no more can the only voice amongst us be one of smart comments and put-downs. We need a newspaper now to take us forward, not hold us back. A newspaper to raise us up, not knock us down.

'Therefore, I am proposing to offer the position of Editor, and access to a not insubstantial amount of money from a special school fund, to whoever can put the best newspaper on my desk by the end of school on Thursday!'

When Mr Chattersly had finished there was a lot of excited murmuring. His big idea had gone down well. I got away before there was any chance I might bump into Julie Singh.

It wasn't as if I actually needed to see the smug look on her face.

Tuesday 15th January

Mr Chattersly's going to be spoiled for choice.

There's going to be loads of completely rubbish

newspapers for him to choose from.

I thought Karl Huck's headlines were bad, but they're masterpieces compared to some of the ones I've heard today. Who knew that 'Tuesday' could be spelled in so many stupid ways?

The only person who worries me is Hari Patel. He can actually write a little bit and he's usually more than happy to let everyone know about it. Norris says he isn't doing anything yet.

That's what worries me.

Norris asked me why I wasn't taking part in the competition.

I had to give him a bit of a speech about the importance of intellectual integrity, free expression and not wanting to write establishment propaganda, but I don't think he was listening properly.

He just said I was chicken.

Ivan the Terrible named Tsar of Russia, 1547

Back when people had proper names.

Hari Patel is definitely up to something.

I was keeping a close eye on him in English. He was
acting strangely. He had this far-away look in his eyes
and every now and again you could see his lips twitch.
It was almost as if he didn't care about how the
writer was using symbolism in *The Rime of the Ancient
Mariner.*

I tried to find him at break, but there was no sign of
him anywhere. Not even in the Creative Writing Club.
It was the same at lunchtime.

I gave up and suggested to Norris that we go and
follow Julie instead. I hadn't seen her around for a bit
either. Normally I can't seem to get away from her,
but it was like she'd vanished.

I told him it would be just like her to take advantage
of all the help I'd given her at *The Woodford Word*
and use it to stab me in the back by trying to start

her own newspaper. Even worse, it would probably be one of those papers telling everyone how fantastic and wonderful they all were.

Norris said maybe Mr Chattersly's competition was making me just a little bit paranoid and I shouldn't forget who my friends are.

I told him that he was desperate for me to fail, just like everyone else, and stormed off.

I think I made my point.

Thursday 17th January

When I got to school, Julie was waiting for me by the gates with Norris and Sally. I reckoned her conscience must finally have caught up with her, so I waited for the apology.

'Hi,' she said, and then stopped.

I waited.

'Oh come on you two, sort it out,' Sally pleaded. 'Just say you're sorry and let's get on with the paper.'

'Just swallow your pride and get it over with,' Norris muttered.

'Get what over with?' I asked.

'The apology,' he said.

'Look, I'm ready whenever she is,' I complained. 'Why don't you tell *her* to get a move on?'

Julie turned to look at Norris and Sally.

That's when I realized they all thought it was me who should have been saying sorry. I couldn't believe it.

'What have I got to be sorry for?' I shouted. 'She's the one who keeps criticizing me.'

'I just wanted you to be a bit more constructive,' Julie said. 'You didn't have to bite my head off.'

'I didn't bite your head off. I just pointed out that I

happen to believe in telling the truth.'

'You were rude, you shouted in my face and you said I couldn't handle the truth.'

'Well, can you?' I asked.

'Well, can *you*?' she asked back.

We were face to face again. Norris and Sally tried to step in between us.

'Can you handle the truth that you're just a trumped-up little nobody who thinks he's better than everyone else?' Julie snarled, stamping on Norris' foot and pushing him out of the way.

'Sure I can!' I yelled back, giving Sally a jab with my elbow. 'Just so long as you can handle the truth that you're an interfering cow!'

I'd have been happy to go on discussing the issue, but we were starting to draw a crowd. I decided to settle the whole matter there and then.

'Listen, as far as I'm concerned, I've got a paper to run and you're either with me or against me. If you're with me, let's go and find out what Hari's up to. If you're not, then leave me alone and let me get on with my job.'

There was an uncomfortable silence.

Then everyone left me alone and let me get on with my job.

I needed a place to think, so I dropped in to the Drop In Zone. It's a room with lots of brightly coloured cushions where you can talk to a teacher about anything that's bothering you.

The place was deserted.

I sat on the funny-shaped cushions and tried to get Julie Singh out of my head. It wasn't easy. The cushions would have been perfect for throwing at her fat interfering face.

I could even hear her voice. It was nagging me about why I was so bothered about Hari. Telling me I was jealous because he'd won a short story competition and that I felt threatened by the fact that he likes to read Shakespeare for pleasure.

I tried to focus. I came to the conclusion that there was no point trying to follow Hari any more. There was only one day left, so he'd probably finished his paper already. That's when I realized I didn't need to find Hari.

I just needed to find his paper.

And a pretty good place to look was probably going to be the big red box marked 'Newspaper Competition' on the table outside Mr Chattersly's office.

A group of Year Elevens were hanging around the

corridor when I arrived, so I pretended to look at some internet safety posters. When they left I made my way over to the red box.

It was full of brown envelopes. I flicked quickly through the top three.

The first two were pretty similar. Cindy Loi had *Well HELLO Woodford* and Kerys Gosforth's effort was called *Way To Go, Woodford*. They both involved people smiling too much.

The third one was from Steven Frost. He hadn't quite mastered the idea of a catchy title, but at least he was letting his readers know exactly what they were going to get with *Steven Frost's Focus on Sport and Music at Woodford School.*

Then I found what I was looking for.

I checked around to see if I was by myself. The coast was clear, but I still made a big show of putting my empty envelope into the box while at the same time sneaking Hari's envelope out. Then I headed for the Drop In Zone.

I opened Hari's envelope carefully so I could tape it back up and replace it when I was done. It felt good to be back in control again. I pulled the paper out.

I don't know what I was expecting, but it wasn't what was in front of me. I flicked through a few pages just to see if they were an improvement on the first, but if anything they were worse. The whole thing was based on a dog called Nifty the News Hound that Hari had tried to make look cool.

He'd tried way too hard.

Nifty had sunglasses, a baseball cap and trousers so low you could see the top of his bum crack.

His hairy bum crack.

If that wasn't bad enough, the name of the paper and every article was written like a speech bubble coming out of Nifty's mouth. There was even a picture of him at the bottom of each page with the slogan '*I've got a nose for news!*'

I flicked to the back pages where Nifty had a sports round-up. At the end of each item there was a *WOOF* rating from one to five for sporting achievement. Everyone scored a five. Even Patrick Raymond, who'd apparently 'battled through difficult circumstances' to lose his badminton match three games to nil.

On closer inspection, the difficult circumstances were that his opponent could play badminton.

I let out a sigh of relief. I admit it; I've been scared I was going to get some proper competition.

What I'm not scared of is a stupid talking dog.

Friday 18th January

For once the school couldn't wait for Mr Chattersly's assembly. Everyone was talking about who was going to win. After lunch I got to the hall early. I wanted to watch all the gory details.

That sure backfired.

Mr Chattersly was early too. He was pacing up and down more than normal. There was a large projector screen pulled down behind him and he tapped a remote control on the palm of his hand.

He looked happy.

Too happy.

As everyone else filed in, I looked out for Hari Patel. I wanted to see his reaction, but I couldn't see him. I could see Julie and Sally quite near me at the front, but they were both determined not to see me.

When the noise had settled down a little, Mr Chattersly paused and reflected for a moment. Everyone else waited for him to get on with it.

When he was done, Mr Chattersly did a massive hair sweep and looked out eagerly over the pupils in front of him.

Too eagerly.

'I'm delighted to see that you're all as excited as I am about our new school newspaper,' he began confidently, 'and I'm pleased to tell you that the winning entry is very exciting indeed. But, before I reveal who has won, I'd like to thank all of you who decided to enter. I've had a most enjoyable time reading over all your efforts. Well done!'

The people who'd entered the competition were surrounded by their friends. Cindy Loi's little clique were giving each other pathetic girl claps and Kerys Gosforth was in the middle of a group hug. Steven Frost's mates were punching him on the arm as hard as they could.

'But there has to be a winner,' Mr Chattersly continued, 'and that winner is...'

Mr Chattersly did a massive pause like on *The X Factor* and pretended he didn't know who the winner of his own competition was. I reckon half the school were expecting glitter cannons to go off.

He stretched the silence to breaking point.

Then all of a sudden it was all over.

'Hari Patel!'

Hari jumped out from behind the curtains at the back of the stage. Despite the lack of glitter, Hari was still keen to big up his big moment. He raised his arms out wide and joined in with the whooping.

Actually, I'm pretty sure he did most of it himself.

Once he'd managed to shut Hari up, Mr Chattersly attempted to calm the school down a little bit.

'Okay, okay, well done Hari,' he said patting at the air with his hands. 'Now then, let's have a look at what Hari's come up with.'

Mr Chattersly pointed the remote control at the projector. I turned my head the other way and got ready to drink in the disappointment in everyone's faces.

That's probably why it took me a while to realize that Nifty the News Hound wasn't there.

Instead there was a picture of a school pupil. One side of him was dressed as a Woodford School pupil in vomit-green blazer and black trousers. The other side of him was dressed in old-fashioned smart brown shoes, long grey socks, grey shorts, grey tank top and a brown peaked cap.

Above the boy was the headline:

WOODFORD NOW AND WHEN

Mr Chattersly gazed out over eight hundred and forty-six faces who were trying to work out if their new school newspaper was brilliant or bonkers. While Mr Chattersly took in the view, Hari picked up the microphone.

'The idea is,' he shouted, 'that we report what's happening *now* in school, as well as what happened back when the school first started. If you turn to page three, for instance, there's an article about how many pupils the school started with compared to how many pupils there are today.'

Mr Chattersly came over to Hari and took the microphone back.

'And the great thing about Hari's idea is that he wants *you* to help him with the research. We know a few things about how Woodford School began but, with

Woodford Now and When, we can all work together and learn a whole lot more. It's inspired!'

As Mr Chattersly went for his hair, Hari grabbed the microphone back.

'I did have another idea: some rubbish about this stupid dog called Nifty the News Hound. I'd just like to apologize to anyone if they got the wrong idea about that.' Hari's eyes sparkled maliciously as he finally gave up the microphone to Mr Chattersly.

Mr Chattersly swept his hair back and did his best sincere face.

'Yes, we were a little worried that Jonny Jakes might try to spoil things, so I'm afraid we put a few decoys in the competition box as well as the real ones. However,' Mr Chattersly continued, 'I'm happy to see that Mr Jakes has decided not to spoil things today and has been gracious in his absence.'

That was the final straw. No one calls me gracious and gets away with it.

_____⚡_____

Sunday 20th January

James Cook discovers the Hawaii Islands
Then he stupidly called them the Sandwich Islands.

It's been a bad weekend.

Yesterday I asked Norris over for a working dinner. He said he needed time to consider whether he wanted to work with me again. I said Dad was going to do pancakes.

'So, what do you reckon?' I asked Norris when I'd finally got him away from the maple syrup.

'Amazing!' he said, shutting his eyes and licking his lips. 'Fluffy and yet somehow gooey at the same time.'

'Not the pancakes, the paper!' I yelled, slapping a copy of

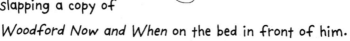

Woodford Now and When on the bed in front of him.

49

'Oh, pretty good I suppose,' he mumbled, picking at his teeth with his fingernails. 'I haven't read it yet.'

'How come it's pretty good if you haven't read it?' I wanted to know.

'It's a clever idea, isn't it? Woodford School now and Woodford School then. Clever.'

'But what are we going to do about it?'

Norris didn't seem to understand the question.

'Nothing.'

'What do you mean, nothing?' I said, trying to keep my voice down. 'We can't just sit here and do nothing.'

Norris picked up Hari's paper and flicked through a few pages. Then he lowered it back down.

'We're not going to do anything about it because there's nothing wrong with it. So *The Woodford Word* has a rival. So what? *You'll* just have to try and make it better.'

'Better? What do you mean?' I protested. '*The Woodford Word* is the best newspaper at Woodford School. Always has been. Always will be.'

'Then there's nothing to be scared of then, is there?' Norris said casually, scraping a stray blob of syrup off his jeans and sticking it back in his mouth.

'I'm not scared of *him*, if that's what you think,' I said, ripping Hari's picture off the back page and thrusting it at Norris.

'Right,' Norris said, smiling even more than usual. 'Sure you're not.'

That's the last time I ask him over for pancakes.

As if Saturday hadn't been bad enough, this morning Dad taught me how to stack the dishwasher. It's going to be my new job.

I've spent the rest of the day mourning the loss of my childhood.

Monday 21st January

I woke up determined not to think about *Woodford Now and When*. I decided to count things instead. I now know that, on average, Mum sighs three times a minute, I chew my breakfast three hundred and twelve times, and there are five hundred and fifty-six white tiles in the bathroom.

Dad decided to use the downstairs toilet in the end.

I was doing well right up until Stephanie Roland burst into the form room. She had the latest edition of *Woodford Now and When* with her. On the front there was a picture of two men staring each other out. One was Mr Chattersly and the other one was this really stern-looking guy called Victory Piggot. Apparently he was the school's first head teacher.

On pages two and three Hari put the head teachers up against each other in a mock contest. Mr Chattersly scored points for not thrashing his pupils with a stick, but Victory Piggot came out top because he had a cooler name and enough facial hair to house a family of squirrels.

Everyone thought it was brilliant and barged in to get a closer look. In fact, there were so many people crowded round, it's a miracle no one was injured when I somehow managed to trip over the table leg and completely shred the paper with the compass I was stupidly waving about in my outstretched hand.

By lunchtime there wasn't anyone without a copy of *Woodford Now and When*. I'd had to get one myself so that I didn't stand out. Norris pretended that's why he had one too, but I think he was just trying to make me feel better.

There were details about how every week 'one lucky reader' would feature in the 'Special Guest' column if they could come up with a good enough article and were prepared to use their real name.

That means two depressing things:

1. Now everyone's going to think they can be a journalist.
2. (And, even worse) everyone's going to keep on buying Hari's paper to see if they're in it.

Tuesday 22nd January

If Hari Patel gets any more big-headed they're going to have to widen the school corridors.

Wednesday 23rd January

By about a mile.

Thursday 24th January

And if he comes into *one* more lesson whooping and high-fiving whoever can't get out of his way quick enough, then I simply won't be responsible for my actions.

Friday 25th January

Henry VIII marries Anne Boleyn in 1533
Three years later he cuts her head off.

The latest edition of *Woodford Now and When* came out this morning.

I could hardly contain my excitement.

'Look at this!' Norris said, waving his copy at me.

'Make me.'

'Read it,' Norris insisted.

'I don't want to read it. I want it to go away.'

'Trust me. You'll want to read this.'

Norris had Hari's paper open to the first special guest reporter's article on page five. It didn't look like he was going to give up, so I took it off him.

'It's got a rubbish title,' I said.

'I know. Keep reading,' Norris replied.

According to the article, Victory Piggot had not only been in the *Rotherby and Woodfordshire Herald* almost every week, but he'd made the national newspapers several times with reports on his pupils' academic achievements and his 'outspoken' remarks on 'the importance of applying radical modern scientific discoveries to the educational establishments of this great country'.

Victory Piggot's Claims to Fame

Former Head Teacher Victory Piggot was something of a minor celebrity. According to our research

There were a couple of grainy old pictures of him from the papers. He was puffing his chest up and trying to look really unhappy.

'Keep going,' Norris instructed.

I read the last three paragraphs. They were annoyingly interesting.

The last time Victory Piggot was big news was in 1872. This time it had nothing to do with his views on education or the outstanding performance of his pupils.

It had a lot to do with him disappearing off the face of the earth.

The article said that, 'despite several investigations', his disappearance was a total mystery. No body was ever found and no foul play was ever suspected. One newspaper had commented:

> The only suspicious circumstance in the disappearance of respected Head Master Victory Piggot is that there are no suspicious circumstances. In previous cases where a prominent individual has disappeared, investigations have usually uncovered probable cause for the disappearance even if they have not discovered the person themselves.

'Okay, I've finished,' I said to Norris, who seemed to be waiting for something.

'No you haven't.'

'How do you know?'

'Because you haven't shouted anything rude yet.'

'Why am I going to shout something rude?' I wanted to know.

'Look at the bottom of the page.'

I looked at the bottom of the page. I shouted something very rude.

You know how sometimes your life is going well and then a girl comes along and spoils it? I thought so.

Julie Singh is Hari Patel's first special guest.

And now, thanks to her story of his mysterious disappearance, Victory Piggot fever is taking over the school. Everyone's got their own theory about what must have happened to him. Mrs McKeane was so excited she used a whole double lesson getting us to write a story about it.

Mine finished with a slow and painful death.

The latest craze is to do an impression of him. It mostly involves crossing your arms, staring like you're in a bad mood and then trying to cane somebody with your pencil case before running away and mysteriously disappearing.

I'm glad it's Friday. My butt cheeks can't take much more.

I asked Norris to come over for a sleepover. Mum said she was glad to see me having fun with my friends for once.

I didn't like to tell her it was a research-based sleepover.

'So, what exactly are we researching?' Norris asked as he booted up his laptop and ripped open three massive bags of sweets.

'Victory Piggot's dirty secrets. What do you think?'

'But what if he was just a really good head teacher?' Norris complained.

'If he was so wonderful, why did he disappear?' I pointed out. 'People disappear when somebody's got something against them or when they're in some sort of trouble.'

Norris grunted something back, but it got lost in a gob-full of gummy bears.

By midnight, the only dirt I had to dish on Victory Piggot was that he wasn't very keen on dogs. In an interview on 21st March 1869 for the *Rotherby and Woodfordshire Herald* he'd been quoted as saying they were 'slavish beasts' who were 'foul germ-carriers of the worst kind'.

Maybe Victory Piggot was murdered by a really angry poodle.

'What have you got?' I asked Norris.

'Hmm?' he mumbled, spreading crumbs from the plate of Jaffa cakes Mum had left on the landing when she'd gone to bed.

'Found anything?' I tried again.

'Oh yeah, look at this game,' he said, turning his laptop to face me. On the screen there was an animation of an old-fashioned classroom with a stern teacher writing questions on a blackboard.

'If you get a question wrong you move back a row,' Norris went on enthusiastically. 'If you get the next one wrong you have to sit in the corner with the dunce's cap. And if you get three wrong in a row you get the cane. Cool, eh?'

'No, it's stupid. We're meant to be looking for something to use against Victory Piggot.'

'I did. There wasn't anything. How about you?' Norris said, and then typed in *1066*. The computer pinged and the teacher beckoned the virtual Norris to come forward.

'Top of the class!' Norris yelled, upsetting his giant tub of toffee popcorn. 'Get in!'

'He didn't like dogs,' I said, when Norris remembered he'd just asked me a question.

'Told you! Nothing,' Norris went on cheerfully. 'This was good, though.' Norris dragged himself away from the game and pulled up something from the bottom of the screen. It was an old drawing of a building with the names *Deakin, Prosper and Flack* at the top.

'What's so good about it?' I asked.

'It's the architect's drawings for Woodford School. The original building. See the date down there? 1848. And look, do you recognize that?'

I crunched across the popcorn and had a closer look. There was a sketch of a lift between the storerooms in the basement and the kitchen above. It looked very familiar.

'The dumb waiter.'

Norris nodded. The dumb waiter was one of the main reasons we'd managed to defeat the evil Mr Jones.

'What's this?' I asked, pointing at a smallish room with lots of writing in the middle. It was further along the corridor from the old storeroom, which was now Miss Briars' still slightly damp drama studio.

'Let's have a look,' Norris said, zooming in. '*Head Teacher's Study*,' he read.

'What's in there now?' I asked.

Norris shrugged. People only went down to the bottom floor and the drama studio if they had drama, and even then they tried not to. It was one of those corridors that didn't exactly encourage you to go any further down it than you had to. It was narrow and cold and damp. And there was some sort of stupid ghost story about it.

I realized that Norris was watching me.

'I dare you,' he said.

I didn't have a good night.

Norris reckons it's because I was thinking about having to go down into the creepy corridor at school on Monday. I told him it was because he snored so much I thought somebody was trying to drill a hole in my head.

I was in a bad enough mood at breakfast without my dad going on about how great it must be having a new school newspaper. Mr Chattersly has put *Woodford Now and When* up on the school website so that parents can read it as well.

Every time Dad said how it must make a nice change from that awful Jonny Jakes, Norris nodded his head in agreement. He could barely control himself when Dad went on about how stupid Jonny's parents must be, and how he'd have worked out what his child was up to months ago.

Sometimes I wonder if I'm adopted.

Monday 28th January

I met Norris outside the drama studio at lunchtime. He looked almost as scared as me.

We didn't say a word as we started along the corridor. It wasn't too bad at first. The light outside the drama studio carried a few metres along, but gradually our shadows started lengthening. We took a turn to the left and then a turn to the right and then the light was all but gone. I pulled a head torch from my bag and put it on.

It looked like nobody had been around for a long time. The corridor was out of bounds to pupils. Judging from the thick layer of dust on the floor and the cobwebs, the cleaners had left it well alone too. If that wasn't creepy enough, the temperature was falling with every step we took.

I did my best not to think about the ghost story.

I tried really hard not to remember that it was about the old school nurse, Mrs Guthrie, who used to work down there and about how, one winter, she got a terrible fever from the boys she looked after.

When that didn't work I started biting the inside of my cheek to try and stop myself thinking about how she was supposed to have died a horrible and agonizing death, screaming for someone to help her.

And when that didn't work I tried to remember the cheat sequence to get up to level six on *Cold Command* so that I wouldn't start imagining her sickly yellow spirit creeping up behind me.

But it was hopeless. When Vanessa Ford had told me the story in Mrs Henrik's biology lesson it had been about as scary as a fake spider. In the corridor I could feel Mrs Guthrie's breath on the back of my neck.

Norris had a printout of the architect's drawing in front of him. We passed some doors, which he counted. Then he stopped in front of a large, black door and nodded.

He put his hand on the door.

'That's weird,' he whispered.

'What is?' I whispered back.

'The door. It's metal.'

'Why's that weird?'

'How many inside doors do you know that are made out of metal?'

I thought about it for a second. I could only think of ones that I'd seen in films.

They usually had something very bad behind them.

Norris gave the door a push but it was locked.

I bent down to have a closer look. Ever since we'd been locked in the drama studio last term, I'd taken steps to avoid it happening again. I'd learned the art of lock picking through a variety of very helpful websites. It was nice to have something to take my mind off being followed by a ghost.

'Solid cast-iron ring lock with keep,' I muttered to myself.

'If you say so,' said Norris.

I pulled out my slimline GN744 Euro Lock Pick from my back pocket. The picks looked like mini instruments of torture as I slid them into the keyhole. It took a few minutes to get the feel of the lock, then a few more and a big squirt of WD40 to get the thing to move.

When I was done I wiped my hands and lifted the latch above the lock. The door screeched open. We froze as the horrible sound rang around the corridor. If there really was a ghost, we'd just woken her up.

I shone the torch all round the room. It was like it had been frozen in time. There was a big, heavy desk, a fireplace with a coal bucket and poker next to it, some old-fashioned cupboards and enough cobwebs to catch about a billion flies.

We went in.

We tried to move carefully, but every step created a big puff of dust. I felt like I'd broken into a tomb.

I pulled at the cobwebs to see what was behind them and they stuck to my blazer. Norris did the same. In a few seconds we looked like something out of *ZombieKILLaz 4*.

The desk was clear and so were the drawers. Norris opened a wooden cabinet and found some empty glass bottles and things that looked a bit like test tubes.

I remembered that Victory Piggot was a keen scientist, and had an image of a mad professor cooking up potions in his laboratory.

It wasn't a particularly helpful image to have in the creepy, cobwebby office of a Victorian head teacher who had mysteriously disappeared.

On the far wall there was an old painting. It was of some big old boring house and it was hanging at an angle. For some reason I reached out and straightened it.

As soon as I touched the painting it crashed to the floor. The cord that had held it up was completely rotten. I shut my eyes as another plume of dust filled the room. When the dust died down I carefully opened my eyes again.

I'd just discovered where Victory Piggot kept his safe.

It was locked. I wiped the front of it with my sleeve. There was a dial with lots of numbers. I had a rough idea that you needed to listen carefully to the clicks as you turned the dial left and right so that you could tell when each part of the lock mechanism was lined up and ready to open.

Norris had a less complicated idea.

'We just need to wedge something in the side of the door and smack it one. Perfect!' he said, as he pulled the big metal poker out from the bucket by the fireplace. 'Now we just need something heavy to hit it with.'

We looked around for something we could use as a hammer. There was a big fat blob of cobwebs on the mantelpiece above the fire. I pulled at them and saw a glimmer of something white beneath them. When I ripped a few more webs off I saw an eye looking back at me.

'Oh, man!

I've just found a skull!' I yelled, backing away in disgust.

'Cool!' Norris said, genuinely pleased.

'It's not cool, it's disgusting! It used to be someone's head!' I pointed out. 'And it's still got an eye!'

'That's not a skull,' Norris said, looking closer. 'That's a bust of someone's head. It's just what we need.'

'Something pretending to be a skull is not just what we need!'

'I mean it's just what we need to hit the poker with,' Norris clarified as he cleaned the rest of the cobwebs off. 'Look, it's Piggot.'

Sure enough, Norris was holding the white, stony face of Woodford School's first head teacher in his huge grubby hands.

Victory Piggot didn't look very happy about it.

'Put the poker in there and hold it still,' Norris said,

as he held the top of the head in his right hand and the bottom plinth thing in his left and lined up the hit. I jammed the poker into the crack between the door and the casing and hoped Norris wouldn't miss.

The door gave up on the fourth attack. It buckled so that, with a little persuasion from the poker, Norris was able to reach in a hand.

'Feels like a book,' Norris said, forcing the gap open wider with his massive forearm. 'Nearly got it.'

He carefully pulled out a small, leather-bound book. It had been protected from the dust so it was easy to read the name on the front in bright gold lettering:

Robert Jennings

Norris was about to open the book but was interrupted by a fit of violent coughing. I wouldn't have minded, but it wasn't him coughing. It was someone else.

Someone else in the haunted corridor.

I switched my torch off and caught a glimpse of a

ghostly yellowish light on the wall outside the study.

I have never stayed so still in my whole life.

The light vanished. As it did there was the faint sound of shuffling feet and I thought I could hear the sound of someone, or something, trying to hold back another cough.

We stayed frozen to the spot for what felt like forever. Neither of us dared to move until the shuffling sounds grew fainter and eventually disappeared. Then, as if from another world, we heard the bell go for the end of lunch. We didn't say a word, didn't even look at each other, as we went all the way back up the stairs.

Outside registration we did our best to brush the cobwebs off each other and blend back in to everyday school life.

It would have worked much better if we hadn't been an hour late and walked into Mad Mean Mr Sheen's general studies A-level class by mistake.

Tuesday 29th January

Some days the biggest excitement is trying to work out what the green things are in your spaghetti bolognese.

Then there's days like today.

I phoned Norris first thing this morning. I'd made him promise not to open the book without me. We didn't manage to look at it last night because he'd had rugby training after school and Mum had forced me to tidy my room.

Next time Norris comes for a sleepover I'm going to make him wear a bib.

We met up in the park on the way to school. Norris pulled the book out of his blazer pocket. He'd wrapped it up in a plastic bag for protection. There was a green sort of ribbon holding the book closed. I realized my hands were sweating as Norris handed the book over for me to open.

So, my readers wanted history? I'd give them history.

And Hari Patel was about to become part of it.

I pulled the ribbon off gently, opened the book at its first page and read the first sentence aloud. It said that the book was:

The diary of Robert Fenwick Jennings

It was a slow start, but the second sentence was a bit more interesting.

For the future well-being of all mankind, please
DO NOT OPEN THIS BOTTLE.

I was about to turn the page when Norris nudged me with his elbow. He nodded across to the far side of the pond. Hari Patel and Julie Singh were walking towards us. They were deep in conversation. There was no way I was going to let them get hold of the diary, so I slipped the book back to Norris and we headed off to school before we were spotted.

The future of mankind was going to have to wait until break.

I could tell we were in trouble as soon as we got to the form room. It's never a good sign when three teachers want to speak to you.

'Those two,' Mr Sheen said, pointing his bony finger at me and Norris.

'Thank you, Mr Sheen, I'll take it from here,' said Mr Chattersly. 'Mark the boys in, Mrs McKeane, and I'll let you know how we get on. This way, boys.'

Mr Chattersly paraded us to his office.

'Sit down,' he instructed when we got there. Me and Norris sank into the two deep leather chairs facing Mr Chattersly's desk.

'Not on the chairs,' Mr Chattersly added, pointing at the floor.

As I strained my neck to try and see over the top of

his desk, Mr Chattersly pulled up something on his computer screen.

'Boys, you've upset Mr Sheen.'

I opened my mouth to explain that everybody upsets Mr Sheen, but Mr Chattersly held up his hand to stop me.

'Now I know that Mr Sheen has, shall we say, a particularly keen interest in upholding some of the more old-fashioned rules of the school,' he said, choosing his words carefully. 'But, on this occasion, he has got a very good point. Indeed, several points.'

Mr Chattersly skim-read what was on the screen in front of him.

'Yesterday you rudely burst into his classroom at

twenty-eight minutes past two, claiming that you thought it was form time. Which, as you well know, finishes at 1.15 p.m. Mr Sheen says that your state of dress was appalling. Top buttons were undone, your ties were covered in cobwebs and, in his own words, you "smelled even worse than most Year Sevens".

'Worst of all, boys, he says that you were plainly lying when he asked you where you had been all this time. Or can you prove,' Mr Chattersly looked meaningfully at us and then back at the computer screen, 'that "Mrs Gelt asked you to help her with her chemistry demonstration on flammable oxides, but it all got a little out of hand"?'

I shot Norris an angry look. That's the last time I let him try and talk us out of trouble.

'Have you anything to say for yourselves?' Mr Chattersly asked.

We shook our heads.

'I thought as much. I take this matter very seriously, boys. Missing lessons is bad enough, but to attempt to deceive a member of staff in such a blatant fashion is beyond the pale. You will spend the rest of the day in my office completing work that your subject teachers have been kind enough to leave you. Mrs Singh will contact your parents and ask them to come in to discuss the matter with me this afternoon. Understood?'

We nodded.

For a second I wondered if it was a good time to mention Robert Jennings' warning, but Mr Chattersly didn't exactly look in the mood for letting us wander downstairs for another look in Victory Piggot's safe.

Instead, me and Norris worked in silence as Mr Chattersly tapped away on his computer keyboard. I tried to catch a reflection of the computer screen in his glasses, but I could only read the title:

Victory Piggot:
A Special Assembly For A Special Man

He was going to read it out this afternoon. At least we were going to miss it.

After an hour, I was still struggling with the French work Madame Le Blanc had set me. The first task was to translate the instructions, but I was pretty sure she didn't want me to bake my horse in the garden.

My brain was saved from meltdown by a knock on Mr Chattersly's door.

'Come,' Mr Chattersly commanded.

One day I want to do that.

'Sorry to bother you, Mr Chattersly,' Mrs Singh said

apologetically as she stuck her head round the door. 'I've phoned both sets of parents and they're happy to come in at two o'clock. Well, when I say happy...'

'I know what you mean, Mrs Singh,' Mr Chattersly smiled. 'Is there anything else?'

'No. Yes. Hang on. What did you want again, pet?' Mrs Singh said, sticking her head back out into the corridor again and speaking to someone we couldn't see. 'Oh yes, and Hari Patel would like to have a quick word. He says it's important.'

At the mention of Hari's name, Mr Chattersly was all smiles.

'Well, if Hari says it's important, it probably is. Tell him I'm just coming.'

Mr Chattersly locked his computer screen and pulled his jacket on. As he left he gave us a hard stare.

'What do you think we should do?' I asked Norris.

'I think we're meant to describe where we live.'

'Not about the French, you idiot! About the possible threat to mankind.'

'What can we do?' Norris shrugged. 'We're stuck in here until our parents arrive. Then they'll ground us forever.'

'Not during assembly. We could check it out then. We've got to find out what's in the bottle. You read what Jennings said.'

'There wasn't a bottle.'

'Look, it was dark, it was creepy, and you only had your hand in that safe for a few seconds. You can't be sure. Get the book out. Let's see if it says anything more about it. If it's just Robert Jennings' idea of a joke, maybe it will say. I'll keep an eye on the door.'

Norris thought about it for a second and then pulled the book out of his pocket again. He flipped to the second page and read it out quietly.

I looked at Norris. He looked back.

If you have discovered this diary and this bottle, then my plan has failed and the future of all God's creatures now rests in your hands. Please, whoever you are, do that which I dared not do. Destroy this bottle and its foul contents!

Again, I beg of you, friend, whatever you do,

DO NOT OPEN THIS BOTTLE.

RFJ

'Well?' I asked.

'You've got to say he's consistent,' Norris admitted.

Norris was about to turn the page when I heard Mr Chattersly say a cheerful goodbye to Hari.

Norris tucked the book up his sleeve just in time.

When he came back, Mr Chattersly kept us hard at it. No breaks. No snacks. No toilet stops. It was torture.

And wondering what Robert Jennings was going on about was doing nothing for my ability to remember how you say 'the most boring place on earth' in French.

At lunch Mr Chattersly asked what we wanted. We put in an order with Mrs Singh for pizza, nuggets and chips, but Mr Chattersly is on a health food drive so we ended up with something that looked like a lawnmower had been emptied on a plate.

When it was nearly two o'clock, Mr Chattersly stopped typing up his speech and printed it off. He looked pleased with himself. Before he left, he gave us a full-on lecture about what would happen if we so much as breathed the wrong way while he was gone.

I might even have paid attention, if he hadn't had a bogey flapping in and out of his nose when he shouted.

When he'd finally left us in peace we counted to sixty before we made our move. The coast was clear so we ran all the way back to Piggot's office.

The big door creaked open. It was pitch black inside and we didn't have time to get torches, so we had to feel our way across the room. Norris tripped over something on the floor. The next second an invisible dust cloud hit us. In the dark we'd forgotten to hold our breath.

I'm not sure my lungs will ever forgive me.

When the hacking and retching and eye-wiping finally died down, Norris went back to heading towards the safe.

'Anything?' I whispered when I figured he'd finally got there.

'Nothing,' came the reply out of the darkness.

'Are you sure?'

'Hang on, there's a bit of paper.'

'Bring it out so we can see it.'

We took a deep breath and stumbled out of the office into the corridor. When we'd got enough light to see our feet again, Norris unfolded the bit of paper.

We could just make out what it said:

> ### Dear Jonny Jakes,
>
> I'm guessing it was you. Thanks for letting me in: I've been wondering what to do about that door for ages! It was very kind of you to open the safe as well.
>
> I can't wait to find out what this stuff actually does.
>
> #### Hari
>
> P.S. Mr Chattersly is <u>particularly excited!</u>

'I've got a bad feeling about Mr Chattersly's special assembly,' I said.

Norris nodded.

We crept carefully through the double doors at the back of the hall. There was still a chance that nothing was going to happen, so we had to be ready to leg it back to Mr Chattersly's office without being noticed.

It was soon obvious that something was up, though. You could tell by the way nobody had fallen asleep.

From the back of the hall, I could just see that Mr Chattersly had a small table on the stage next to him. On it was a small bottle.

Keeping our heads down, me and Norris nudged our way nearer.

We stopped a couple of rows from the front and I pulled my spy telescope out of my pocket. It looks just like a biro. I put it to my eye and adjusted the focus.

The writing on the bottle's label was fancy and loopy, like the writing in Robert Jennings' diary. What it said was just as interesting.

I gave Norris the telescope
to check I wasn't seeing things. His jaw dropped open.

I began to register what Mr Chattersly was saying.

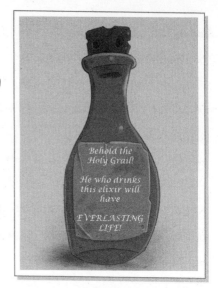

Behold the
Holy Grail!

He who drinks
this elixir will
have

EVERLASTING
LIFE!

'Of course, it's all complete nonsense,' he chuckled. 'The quest for the Holy Grail has fascinated people for centuries and dear old Victory Piggot is just another mere mortal obsessed with the idea of eternal life. And so, to put my money where my mouth is, and just to prove that you shouldn't always take your head teacher too seriously, I am going to drink what is in this bottle. After all,' he smiled, flicking his hair and winking, 'if I'm wrong, what's the worst that can happen?'

Everyone laughed.

A cold sweat broke out on the back of my neck. I realized that Norris wasn't next to me any more. I looked to see where he'd gone. He was pushing his way to the steps at the side of the stage.

Mr Chattersly picked up the ancient bottle. He was loving all the attention and turned to pose with it for Hari, who was taking his picture for another front page.

Norris had made it onto the steps, but all eyes were on Mr Chattersly, who was pulling the cork out of the bottle.

'Cheers!' he said as Norris pounded, still unnoticed, towards him.

Just as the bottle touched Mr Chattersly's lips, it paused. His smile had vanished and through the telescope I could see that his hand was shaking slightly.

Maybe it was a dramatic pause. Maybe it was second thoughts. I'll never know, because my view was suddenly obscured by Norris flying through the air screaming 'NOOOO!' at the top of his voice and rugby-tackling Mr Chattersly to the floor.

In a split second the mood turned from excitement to

terror. Everyone was stunned and a few people couldn't stop shrieking. Norris got to his knees and stared at the crumpled figure he'd left on the floor. He looked like he couldn't believe what he'd done.

The whole hall held its breath and waited to see if Norris had just killed their head teacher.

Eventually a low groan came from the heap on the floor. With one hand rubbing his head, Mr Chattersly sat up. In the other hand he was still clutching the bottle. It hadn't smashed and amazingly it still looked almost full.

Norris heaved a sigh of relief.

Suddenly Mr Chattersly's free hand started to clutch at his throat. His eyes bulged and watered and he started shaking like someone having a fit. One of the teachers rushed forward and grabbed the bottle out of his hand.

Norris tried to hide behind the table.

As quickly as it had started, Mr Chattersly's shaking stopped. His eyes stopped bulging and his shoulders relaxed. He started patting himself all over as if he was checking he was still there. He flapped his ears backwards and forwards, stretched his mouth open and flicked his tongue up and down. Then he opened and shut his eyes repeatedly.

Satisfied that his face worked, he got to his feet. He looked down at them for a bit, like he hadn't seen them before. Then he inspected his hands. He put one of them in front of his mouth and breathed on it. A large grin spread across his face.

Then he looked at us.

'What are you all staring at?!' he bellowed.

Everyone in the hall wondered if their ears were playing tricks on them. It wasn't just because it wasn't the sort of thing Mr Chattersly usually said. It wasn't even because he was acting so aggressively all of a sudden.

It was because Mr Chattersly didn't sound anything like Mr Chattersly.

'And what on earth are you all wearing? And what-'

Suddenly Mr Chattersly's whole body shook and there was a massive gasp as Mr Chattersly's voice changed back to its normal, less ear-shredding tone.

'Er, hi. Alistair Chattersly, pleased to meet you,' he said.

To himself.

His body shook again.

'Alistair Chattersly? What sort of ridiculous name is that?' the booming voice answered. 'Where's Robert?'

'Which one?'

'My prefect, you gibbering fool!'

'Er, well, Robert Preston is on the school council,' the original voice of Mr Chattersly informed himself. 'Give our visitor a little wave, Robert, so he can see who you are.'

Robert Preston couldn't have looked more confused if someone had smacked him around the head with a wet fish and asked him what ice cream he wanted with his chips. In the end he decided it was probably best to give Mr Chattersly a little wave.

'You're not Robert, you insolent boy! Report to my office immediately!' Mr Chattersly thundered before looking around the hall as if he'd never seen the place before. 'What have you done with it?'

Mr Chattersly shook violently again.

'There's nothing to be worried about, children,' the usual voice of Mr Chattersly said as calmly as it could manage. 'But it seems like our little experiment has gone slightly wrong.'

'I couldn't agree more!' the loud voice agreed. 'You, sir, have the mind of an imbecile, the hair of a woman, and what have you done to my school? It looks abominable!'

'Ah, well, you see, there are bound to have been some changes. After all, it is the twenty-first century.'

Mr Chattersly shook one final time and took in his surroundings with an expression of great distaste.

'We'll see about that!' he bellowed and stormed off.

When we'd recovered from the shock, me and Norris raced back to Mr Chattersly's office, working on the assumption that at least some of him might have remembered about us.

When we got there we quickly pulled a few books in front of us and pretended to work.

It was a few minutes before Mr Chattersly appeared. He was still arguing with himself as he came in. Apparently someone had dropped a crisp packet on the stairs.

'It's a disgrace! I want the culprits identified and punished immediately! Where do you keep your cane?'

'I'm afraid we don't do things like that any more.'

'What are you wittering on about, you dim-witted fool? You mean to say you don't beat the students? How on earth do you maintain discipline?'

'Well, we have a more collaborative approach. Of course there are detentions, but we prefer to talk to the pupils and try to make them understand what they've done wrong.'

'A throbbing backside lets them know perfectly well when they've done something wrong and...'

Mr Chattersly had realized that he wasn't alone in his office. He glared at us fiercely and I had no doubt about what half of him wanted to do with us.

Luckily the other half slid back into place.

'Ah yes. You two. I think, in the circumstances, we'll skip the interview with your parents. They will, however, take you home now and this will be marked down on your school record as a half-day suspension for rude behaviour and an unforgivable lapse in punctuality. Now run along.'

We rushed out of the door just as Mr Chattersly's more violent side returned and started looking round for something to hit us with.

After Mrs Singh explained that Mr Chattersly was unavoidably detained, my parents drove me home in silence. I got sent to my room without any tea. My dad said he wasn't going to talk to me until I'd had time to think very carefully about what I'd done.

It was the best news I'd had all day.

Wednesday 30th January

My parents still aren't talking to me. I think they're trying to show how disappointed they are. And I don't think Norris will be welcome for another sleepover anytime soon. Mum passed me a note over breakfast saying I wasn't to have anything to do with him for the rest of the week.

When I met him at the park, Norris told me his parents had said the same.

He had big rings under his eyes. His mum had made him turn his lights out early, so he'd had to wait for them to go to sleep before he got started on the diary.

I asked him what it was like. He said it was pretty boring at first but it got going after a while and when I got to the bit about 'How to Safely Turn Living Tissue into Viable Fluids' I'd probably throw up. He reckoned Mr Chattersly was now half Mr Chattersly and half Victory Piggot.

I said I'd worked that out for myself, but why was that such a bad thing for the future of all God's creatures? He gave me the diary and told me to find out for myself.

Hari Patel's put out another issue of *Woodford Now* and

THE PAST SPRINGS BACK TO LIFE

When. He managed to get a brief interview with our new-look head teacher, but it was cut short when the Victory Piggot part of him apparently threatened to pull Hari's liver out through his throat if he didn't stop poking his nose in where it didn't belong.

It's been a strange day. Mr Chattersly/Victory Piggot have pretty much stayed in his/their office trying to sort his/their/its difference(s) out. No one knows what's going to happen next, and I have absolutely no idea about the correct use of pronouns in this situation.

Everyone realizes that drinking some of the bottle did something really weird to Mr Chattersly, but there's been loads of arguments about exactly what it was. Everyone who believes in ghosts is telling everyone who doesn't they told them so. Everyone who doesn't believe in ghosts is telling everyone who does to shut up while they try and come up with a better explanation.

There's some pretty smug believers in the supernatural out there.

Thursday 31st January

It's stupid o'clock.

I've been reading Robert Jennings' diary and I can't sleep. I now know two very important things:

1   Victory Piggot is definitely alive and well over one hundred years after his mysterious disappearance.

2   He's a complete nutter.

Looks like I've got a new enemy.

It was a bit confusing to start with. The first two pages, the ones I'd already seen, had obviously been written after everything else. Once you got past those, the diary started explaining it all from the very beginning.

Like Norris said, it was pretty boring at first. Robert Jennings had really small handwriting and kept using words like *forthwith*. It did my head in, but I kept going.

He started Woodford School in 1865. His dad had sent him because he wanted his son to be *at the forefront of the great scientific age* and reckoned that Victory Piggot was exactly what his son needed. He told Robert to work hard.

At first, Robert was totally obedient. He wrote that he was *most eager to please both my father and illustrious Head Master*. It got worse. Soon he was putting in stuff like *Mr Piggot held our minds firmly in his grasp* and *Once again Mr Piggot shone light where before there were only shadows*.

I nearly had to get a bucket.

Although he was really strict with the other boys, for some reason Victory Piggot went easy on Robert. There seemed to be some sort of bond. He only caned him once and even then, Robert said, *the strokes fell lightly across my buttocks.* Maybe it was because Piggot wanted someone to *further discuss his fascinating philosophy* with, or maybe it was because Robert was such a massive creep.

Either way, when he was *invited to assist the Head Master in his own private research* Robert Jennings was one seriously happy bunny.

After a hard day's corporal punishment, Piggot liked nothing more than telling Robert about how they were living in a *Golden Age of Discovery.* There was a load of science stuff about microscopes and bacteria that I didn't really get. Then he ranted on about *damn foreigners* like *Robert Koch* and *Louis Pasteur meddling where they didn't belong.* Apparently they were figuring out how germs carried diseases and generally trying to turn the world into a healthier place.

Piggot insisted that if the world really wanted to know how diseases worked, it was going to be the British and Victory Piggot who told them.

He asked Robert if he wanted to help him in his work. Robert replied that he would be *delighted and honoured to have the privilege of pursuing so noble a purpose.*

Soon Robert was hard at work in the laboratory putting horrible things in animals to see what would happen to them.

Basically, they died.

There's a lot more detail in the diary but if you haven't got a mop handy it's probably best not to go into it.

One day Victory Piggot was majorly excited. He invited Robert into his office to show him why.

It was a great honour to be invited into the Head Master's office. Normally boys are only allowed to enter for reasons of punishment. I thought how proud my father would be if he could have seen me.

About the shelves Mr Piggot had arranged an impressive collection of jars and so forth.

The labels were in Mr Piggot's own fine hand but he used symbols and shorthand that, in my ignorance, I could only guess at.

In a state of much excitement, Mr Piggot pulled down two of these jars and then, from beneath his desk, two small cages. In one cage was a rabbit, in the other a wren.

'Watch this,' he cried, eyes sparkling.

Into the rabbit's cage he placed a lettuce leaf. The rabbit, on spying the leaf, set to it in vigorous fashion. Then a spider was placed in the wren's cage and the bird responded likewise.

'You see?' Mr Piggot enquired, with such enthusiasm and beads of excited perspiration on his brow that I wondered if he had temporarily lost control of his faculties.

After all, I had only seen a rabbit eating a lettuce leaf and a wren eating a spider, and what was so remarkable about that?

'Yes sir, I see,' I replied, not knowing quite what else to do.

Mr Piggot sensed my predicament.

'Be patient, Robert, the best is yet to come.'

Mr Piggot picked up the jar on his right and drew a syringe full of the dark liquid therein; this he injected into the rabbit. He repeated the procedure with the liquid in the jar on his left, only this was injected into the wren.

At first, both animals seemed unaffected by the experience, but then I noticed that the rabbit was less and less concerned with the lettuce leaf and the wren less and less concerned with devouring the spider.

I shall never forget it stopping, mid-meal, with three hairy legs still hanging out of the side of its beak.

Mr Piggot then brought out another lettuce leaf and another spider, only this time the rabbit got the spider and the wren the lettuce leaf. In an instant both of the creatures' appetites were restored and I was left very much amazed.

Somehow Victory Piggot had made an amazing breakthrough. Through researching the transfer of germs, he had also learned how to transfer behaviour from one animal to another.

From that day on, Robert Jennings was put to work swapping all sorts of animal behaviour: sparrows tried to dig a nest in the ground, rats thought they could lay eggs, and frogs tried to fly. There was usually a lot of cleaning up afterwards.

For a couple of years, Robert Jennings and Victory

Piggot were like the sorcerer and his apprentice and everything was good.

Not for the animals, obviously.

Then things started to change. Piggot got more secretive. He spent far less time roaming the school looking for excuses to hurt people. Robert was invited into Piggot's office less and less. When he was allowed in, he noticed that the labelling system, which he'd finally got the hang of, had changed again. There were symbols and equations he couldn't find in any of the regular textbooks and which his master was reluctant to explain.

The animals changed too. Instead of mice and frogs and birds, Piggot was keeping larger animals. Cats and dogs stared mournfully out of their cages.

Then, on 23rd November 1869, Robert Jennings seriously freaked out. I don't blame him.

A morning I will never forget.

Master Spencer was conducting our Latin revision, as was the custom on a Friday. My mind, I confess, was wandering as he conjugated the verb morir for what felt like the umpteenth time. Instead of chanting back, I was gazing through the window, listening to the trill of a starling as it enjoyed its freedom beyond my gloomy classroom.

The pleasant birdsong was suddenly interrupted by the clamour of a dog's bark.

I wondered what had caused the dog to bark and which of the town's remaining mongrels the offending noise belonged to. There has been a stir in the local newspaper recently about a number of household pets having gone missing, and the sound of a dog barking has become something of a rarity.

My musings were interrupted by a sharp elbow in my ribs. I turned in my chair to remonstrate with my neighbour, but all thoughts of revenge were banished when I saw our prefect and realized that the barking was not, after all, coming from without.

It was coming from him.

It was not thirty seconds later when the lesson was interrupted by the appearance of Mr Piggot. His face was flushed and red from exertion and, I believe, a sense of panic. Peter Spencer was swiftly removed by means of his ear lobe and we were told to get on with our work and dispel our prefect's foolishness immediately from our minds.

In that moment Robert realized why Piggot had been keeping so quiet. His classmates may have thought that Peter Spencer had been messing about, but Robert knew differently.

He knew that Victory Piggot was no longer just trying his experiments out on animals.

Peter Spencer was rarely seen again. The boys were told he had a tropical fever and needed to be confined to his bed. One time Robert said he was allowed down to breakfast and *appeared to be his normal self again*.

Then he weed on a table leg.

Robert noticed changes in the other boys. Edward Knight's limp kept swapping legs. Benjamin Hines, the worst mathematician at the school, finally learned his multiplication tables. Overnight. And, Henry Dent, a boy who *couldn't be trusted to put his trousers on the right way round*, one day amazed everyone by *catching an absolute snorker at second slip*. Apparently that's a really good thing in cricket.

This sort of stuff went on for a year. During his holidays Robert tried to explain what was going on to his father, but he took no notice. Robert started complaining that his father didn't understand him and that all his parents were interested in was whether he was doing all right at school.

Finally he was speaking my language.

It was in his seventh and final year that Robert was once again invited in to Piggot's office. He didn't want to go but he knew he had no choice. Besides, he had made his mind up that Piggot couldn't be allowed to continue, and it was up to him to stop him.

On entering the office I was relieved to see that there were no longer any more cages harbouring those poor, unfortunate creatures. My guard was up, though, the moment Mr Piggot turned to face me.

Even since the end of last term his appearance had changed dramatically. His features had become pinched and lined, and his eyes held a special light only to be found in those in a high attitude of fear, desperation or lunacy.

'Ah, Robert. I have neglected you, I know. But the demands of progress have to be met! And Robert, I have made much progress!'

These last words were said with such a manic conviction that I could feel the hairs rise up on the back of my neck. Every natural urge in my body was telling me to leave this madman alone, but I knew I could only better him if he still believed he had my confidence.

I beseeched him to inform me further and did my utmost to once again play the part of the eager apprentice.

'Patience, Robert. I know you desire to know more and you shall not be disappointed, but there are a few more steps I must take, and which I must take alone. Attend on me at this hour, on this day, a month from now and your faith in me shall have its just reward.'

So that's what Robert did.

If you've just had your tea, I suggest you read this bit later.

I returned to Mr Piggot's office exactly one month later, as he had bid me do. As I knocked on the door, I prepared my features so that my feelings of disgust and revulsion should once again be hidden by a mask of feigned interest.

At first my knocking received no reply, so after a polite pause I tried again. This time the familiar voice replied.

'Is that Robert?'

I assured him that it was.

'Are you alone?'

Again I answered yes. Then the voice boomed again.

'Come.'

For a few moments after I opened the door I was unable to distinguish anything in the room I had just entered. The first shapes that came out of the gloom were those of the desk and chair. Then gradually I began to make out the form of Mr Piggot. His white, whiskery sideburns seemed to be floating in the blackness.

I stood before the silent figure, more scared than I have ever been before, but more determined than ever that whatever the monster in front of me was planning to do, it must be stopped tonight.

An oil lamp on the desk flickered into life. It was painful to my eyes, having just become accustomed to the dark. When I could see clearly again I noticed that although the light reached me, some sort of shield behind the lamp was preventing the light from falling on Mr Piggot, so that he remained an outline only.

I could feel myself being inspected.

'I'm sorry about all this, Robert, but you will soon see why I have to be so sure. You are about to become the beneficiary of all my years of research. If you do exactly as I say, in a matter of minutes you will become the most famous, the most celebrated man to have ever lived.

'My dear boy, you will live forever.'

I had no reply to give to this. What reply could there be?

'It is time,' the dark shape commanded eventually. 'Attend me carefully, or these will be the last words you ever hear me say. What is about to happen will be very unpleasant. You may wish to close your eyes. But when it is over, there is one thing you must do. Do you understand me, Robert?' This last was snapped, and there was a sense of desperation once more in Mr Piggot's manner.

I nodded and he appeared to be satisfied.

'In front of you, there will appear, in a short time, a bottle. All you have to do is drink it.'

I nodded again. I confess that I could not prevent myself from a small sob of fear.

'You have served me well, Robert. Do this final act for me and all will be well. I promise. Now shut your eyes.'

It began with a grunt and wheezy breathing, as of an old man under some horrible duress. Then, a stifled scream. Then ... it was as if the room itself were dissolving. In a terrible panic I blinked open my eyes, just to make sure there was still ground for me to stand on. I regretted it soon enough.

The shape that had been my Head Master had become some sort of bubbling, heaving mass. It was as if a barrel of tar had somehow come to life. There were eyes, but they were liquid and fathomless. There was a neck, but it coiled and lengthened and looped until it was impossible to tell head from body or body from head.

A terrible screech from the cavernous mouth made me shut my eyes again, and now a frothing, fermenting gurgle tormented my ears, accompanied by the foulest of stenches. I tried my hardest not to succumb to the burning sensation in my forehead and the sickening numbness everywhere else, but I did not succeed.

The last thing I remember was a fearsome whooshing sound, as if everything was being sucked from the room.

When I came to, the room swam before my eyes. As it began to come back into focus, I could see that the black shape behind the desk had disappeared.

In its place, bearing a strange label, was a small bottle.

Sweet dreams.

Norris didn't have to ask me if I'd read the diary. He saw the bags under my eyes and just nodded.

'So what do we do?' he asked.

'What we always do,' I replied. 'Tell the truth.'

'What if no one believes it?'

'That's their problem.'

And by the look of it, it's going to be a big problem.

Mr Chattersly and Victory Piggot have worked out their issues. Well, Piggot has worked out his. Mr Chattersly is going to do exactly what he tells him to.

I was on the way to biology when I heard footsteps come up behind me. The next thing I knew, something heavy smacked me on the back of the head.

'That's the way to do it, Chattersly,' boomed the voice of Victory Piggot. 'Let them know who's in charge.'

I watched with stars in my eyes as Mr Chattersly's body marched past me. It was swinging a massive German dictionary in its hand and making a bunch of Year Nine girls run for cover. Victory Piggot was in an unpleasantly good mood.

'You see that? Respect! That's what that is, Chattersly. I'll soon have this school working properly again.'

By lunchtime I could see that it's not just that the school is being run by a violent maniac that we need to worry about.

It's more the fact that everybody seems to like it.

'It was pure class in religion,' George Murray informed us in afternoon registration. 'Chattersly came in to Watson's lesson. He told everyone to stand up and then asked them questions. He asked me to list ten differences between Christianity and Judaism. I only got to three, so he smacked me seven times on the hand with a ruler. Look at the blisters on that!'

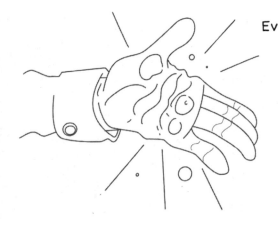

Everyone agreed they were well impressive and couldn't wait to get some of their own.

Hari is going to get another interview, only this time it looks like Piggot might be warming to the publicity. He told everyone in assembly that his reappearance would be properly explained to them in tomorrow's issue of *Woodford Now and When*, along with the publication of a new set of school rules.

Oh joy.

The rest of the assembly mostly involved him lecturing us about 'standards', 'discipline' and how we were all 'snivelling little brats'. It went down really well.

To finish off, he made us all sing.

He's got to go.

Friday 1st February

It would be a lot easier to defeat Victory Piggot if I didn't feel like a total zombie. I tried to get going on the comeback issue of *The Woodford Word* last night, but I fell asleep at my laptop.

You can still see the % sign on my forehead.

I'm so tired I can't think straight. I can't even eat properly. I nearly drowned in my own cereal this morning. Mum kept asking me if there was anything wrong, but I didn't know where to start.

I was almost too tired to take any notice of the new edition of *Woodford Now and When*. Unfortunately Norris pointed it out in registration. He also pointed out that Hari's interview had made it onto the front page of practically every national newspaper, along with his headline:

WOODFORD NOW AND WHEN

Two Heads are Better Than One

VICTORIAN HEAD TEACHER RETURNS TO DO HIS DUTY

In another extraordinary world first, Woodford School has found itself with a new head teacher. Or should we say *teachers*.

The school is crawling with reporters. Everyone's desperate to get interviewed and give their opinion on what it's like to have their head teacher possessed by the spirit of a mad Victorian.

It's not an opportunity that comes along very often.

Julie had another article in. This time she'd written about how much better standards of behaviour were back when 'children knew their place' and how Victory Piggot's influence could be a real boost to 'improving youngsters' behaviour'.

It confirmed my long-held belief about anyone who uses the word 'youngster'.

The new school rules took up the rest of the paper.

Basically, you can't do anything.

The other teachers are terrified of Piggot. They all try and keep out of his way. This morning he was so busy twisting Michaela Grey's ear for daring to look him in the eye that he smacked Mr Hamilton in the face with his elbow. Mr Hamilton apologized and said it wouldn't happen again.

Michaela Grey couldn't wait for everyone to see how badly her ear lobe was bleeding.

At the end of the day Norris wanted to know the plan of action. I said that we were going to work our butts off over the weekend. In particular, we were going to make sure we let the world know that Victory Piggot was an evil mad scientist and shouldn't be trusted.

He said what about the fact that our parents still didn't want us to see each other?

I said what about it?

Saturday 2nd February

My much-needed lie-in was ruined by the familiar sound of Victory Piggot.

And the unbelievable hypocrisy of my parents.

Apparently it *is* okay to have the TV blaring away first thing in the morning, *as long* as you're watching an interview with a lunatic who's demanding the death penalty for teenagers who show their pants off in public.

I thought I was safe when my parents went shopping but it turns out that Victory Piggot has already become a high street brand. They came back with Victory Piggot tea towels, a Victory Piggot pencil case, a set of Victory Piggot eggcups and a Victory Piggot dressing gown my mum bought especially for my dad. It's got a picture of Victory Piggot looking even more angry than usual and waving a cane.

Dad liked it so much, he put it on straight after dinner.

As if my digestive system needed any more aggravation.

Sunday 3rd February

Me and Norris have been working on *The Woodford Word* all day. I stockpiled food yesterday and sneaked him into my room early this morning before there was any chance of meeting the dressing gown.

The only interruptions were Mum and Dad, who kept shouting for me to come down. They wanted me to read all the special Victory Piggot supplements in the Sunday papers.

I've stopped twice. Once to write this and once to accidentally spill orange juice all over the Victory Piggot supplements in the Sunday papers.

Monday 4th February

The Woodford Word was back in business first thing in the morning.

There was the headline:

THE WOODFORD WORD

THE SHAME OF VICTORY PIGGOT

Victory Piggot, the man of the moment, owes his reappearance to a dark and dreadful secret

There was the expert witness with the in-depth, inside story, exposing the secrets of Victory Piggot's gruesome past:

> *I regret to write, dear diary, that it is clear to me now that Victory Piggot is one of the most dangerous men to have ever lived.*

And, just in case the extracts from Robert Jennings' diary didn't do the trick, there were lots of pictures of fluffy animals looking sad.

Nobody likes a man who's mean to bunny rabbits.

I made sure the reporters hanging around the school got a copy and left a note under Mr Bream's desk letting my fellow pupils know where they could get theirs. I even left a pile outside the staffroom.

By nine o'clock I expected to be sold out. By break time I expected a riot. By the end of the day I expected Victory Piggot to be gone.

They say two out of three isn't bad.

One out of three sucks.

The selling-out bit wasn't a problem. Victory Piggot's name could sell a pile of pus at the moment. The problem is, I've made him more popular than ever.

'Legend!' George Murray cried as he came into the form room waving *The Woodford Word* above his head. 'Have you seen this? He turned a pupil into a dog!'

'Class!' Syfur Dravid agreed, flicking through his copy. 'And look at this! He made frogs think they could actually fly.'

'Suicidal frogs! Mega-class!'

'Sick!'

Syfur attempted to do an impersonation. It mostly involved him jumping off a chair going, 'Ribbit! Splat!'

Over and over again.

As for the riot, most pupils spent their break time drawing pictures of mutated animals on their school bags and working on a new set of Victory Piggot catchphrases.

Even the reporters didn't seem that bothered about Piggot's past. I heard one reporter on his mobile. He was telling someone to mock up some pictures of mixed-up animals and going on about how Victory Piggot was way ahead of his time.

The only group of people who are showing any sort of sense are the teachers. Ironic or what? They usually avoid *The Woodford Word* like the plague, so I was surprised to see that the pile of papers outside the staffroom had almost disappeared.

I'll make sure they have to pay for it next time.

The teachers might be scared of Victory Piggot, but that doesn't mean they have to like him. Miss Briars was particularly upset. She's the completely mad but surprisingly violent drama teacher who helped us defeat Mr Jones. She gave a television interview saying that she was worried about the 'mixed moral message' pupils might be getting from their new head teacher.

Although Piggot was by no means gone, he was at least keeping a low profile. I only saw Chattersly once, on the way to history. He was muttering something to Hari, who was walking a step behind him, taking notes.

I met Norris at the end of school. I needed some answers.

'I don't get it. Where did we go wrong?' I asked him.

'I guess people love eccentrics,' he replied.

'But he's not eccentric! He's a nutter!'

'I'm not sure most people know the difference,' Norris reckoned cheerfully. It takes more than a maniac to get Norris down.

A group of Year Eights with their arms out of their coats swarmed past. They were doing their own frog impressions.

'Well, I'm going to have to teach them then,' I muttered, watching them pass by.

We walked on in silence. For some reason Norris had lost his smile.

About time.

Tuesday 5th February

As I got close to the school gates this morning, the mutter of angry voices drifted my way. It was strange. They sounded less like disappointed teenagers than usual.

Then I saw why. Underneath their cheap suits and bad jewellery, the teachers had got in touch with a part of themselves they hadn't used for a long time.

Their spines.

It wasn't just Miss Briars who was prepared to make a stand against her new boss now. The playground was filled with teachers carrying banners. They said things like:

MORALS MAKETH A MAN

FOR UNTO WHOMSOEVER MUCH IS GIVEN, OF HIM SHALL BE MUCH REQUIRED!

Some of them even made sense.

The pupils were loving it. Everyone was taking pictures.
The reporters who were still around were lapping it up
too.

'Er, hi.'

I turned to see who had tapped me on the shoulder.

'Shouldn't you have taken a few pictures?' Julie Singh
nodded at the teachers, who were beginning to march
back into the school. She held her hands up. 'Not that
I'd try and tell you how to do your job.'

'I did,' I replied. Less crossly than I expected. 'I've
got a camera here...' I pointed at the button camera on
my blazer. 'It looks just like a button,' I added.

Julie nodded. I waited for the 'told you so' or at least
some mention of TWW's recent epic fail. For some
reason it didn't arrive. Julie just stared at the button
camera. I couldn't think of anything else to do so I
tried to do the same.

All it needed was someone to say 'awkward'.

At break time, the teachers were at it again. Their chants were growing bolder.

'Piggot, Piggot, Piggot, you really ought to think carefully about what you've done,' squeaked the nervous chemistry teacher whose name everyone forgot.

'Victory P isn't for me!' called out Mr Grieve, impressed with his rhyme.

'Piggot! Piggot! Piggot! Out! Out! Out!' yelled Miss Briars in full flow.

It was a beautiful scene and it got even prettier when Mr Chattersly/Victory Piggot was forced to come out. Instantly a load of microphones were thrust in his face. He did his best to act like he wasn't bothered about all the fuss, but his forehead was tense and his eyes looked tired.

'All right, all right, you've made your point!' Mr Chattersly said, back in his normal voice. It sounded quiet and strange.

'Piggot! Piggot! Piggot! Out! Out! Out!' the teachers replied.

Mr Chattersly had to increase the volume.

'Alright! I can hear you! Mr Piggot has agreed to talk to you in the staffroom at the end of the day! But only if you go back to your lessons now!'

The teachers huddled together and did a bit of mumbling. Miss Briars found herself nudged to the front.

'And has he decided to leave?' she asked.

Mr Chattersly squirmed and tried to control his inner Piggot. Hari whispered in his ear.

'He has decided to consider his position,' Mr Chattersly told the mob.

The teachers muttered briefly amongst themselves again.

'Alright,' Miss Briars said, looking Mr Chattersly squarely in the eye. 'As long as he considers it very carefully.'

It was a weird afternoon. No one really knew what to do. Bells went. Pupils shuffled in and out of classrooms. Teachers talked.

Everyone watched the clock.

At 3.30 p.m. the bell went for the end of the day but no one was ready to go home. The teachers descended on the staffroom and the pupils and reporters waited outside and tried to work out ways of listening to what was being said behind the closed doors. It mostly involved going 'Sshh!' every two seconds.

By 4 p.m. a lot of people had given up and the crowd in the corridor was thinning. By 5 p.m. we still hadn't heard a thing. The only excitement had been the dinner ladies taking a load of drinks and biscuits in. It wasn't much to base a story on.

At 6 p.m. we gave up. It was either that or miss *Monster Truck Mash-Up*, and there was no way I was giving up my weekly fix of mechanized violence for a story about a drinks trolley and a bunch of bourbons.

Wednesday 6th February

I set my alarm clock for 5.30 a.m. so me and Norris could get into school first thing. I wanted to capture every last bit of a Piggot-free day. The plan was spoiled, however, about ten seconds after 5.30 a.m. when the alarm clock was the victim of an act of violence from which it didn't recover.

My mum woke me up three hours later.

When I got to school, Norris was waiting for me at the gates. He was looking smug.

'And I thought *I* was late.'

'Alarm clock malfunction,' I informed him.

'You too?' he grinned.

'Come on.'

We headed straight for the staffroom but we didn't get very far. The second we stepped into the building, the fire alarm went.

We piled into the yard along with the rest of the pupils and lined up in our forms. No one knew what the state of play with Piggot was, so no one was taking any chances messing about.

When the alarm stopped there was a strange silence. This was usually the point where the teachers either took the register, told you off for not being smart enough, or did both at the same time. But all you could hear was the wind, pushing at the trees on the edge of the playground. There wasn't a teacher to be seen.

The silence lingered.

And the longer the silence stayed, the more no one felt they could break it. And the longer no one felt they could break it, the more everyone wished someone would. Pretty soon it became the sort of silence that made someone invent the word 'eerie'.

That's when we heard the laughter.

I tried to work out where it was coming from. It seemed to be coming from everywhere and nowhere at the same time. It was cruel and hard and reminded me of Patrick Docherty frying ants with a magnifying glass.

The whole school was wheeling round on the spot, desperate to get a fix on the noise. Manic laughter is bad enough. Manic laughter that's somehow everywhere but coming from nowhere makes you wonder if you're going completely bonkers.

'Over there!' someone shouted, pointing towards the science block.

We all turned to look. Sure enough, a procession of dark-cloaked figures was coming around the edge of the science block towards us.

I shivered.

It wasn't just the black cloaks. It wasn't even the horrible sense of purpose with which they were moving, although that didn't help. It was the way they all marched so completely and utterly in time. I felt like someone had nailed me to the spot.

With fence posts.

As the procession got closer it got a bit less terrifying. The manic laughter stopped and the cloaks began to look a bit less Batman and a bit more like the sort of thing that old-fashioned head teachers used to wear.

The mystery of the missing teachers was starting to clear up too.

Our form tutors took up their usual positions at the front of the lines, their dusty black gowns billowing behind them. The rest of the teachers faced us, with their backs to the main school building. I waited for Mrs McKeane to call the register, but she just stared at a point above my head. She was waiting for something.

Then something happened.

The big blue door that led out from the main building started to open. The teachers in front of the door parted to form two neat lines leading towards the playground. In the doorway stood a man.

Not a tall man, not a wide man, but a man who had worked out how to stand so that a thousand people couldn't take their eyes off him. He stood like a man with a broomstick for a backbone. Like a man who expected to have statues made of him. Like a man born to rule.

If he'd tilted his chin up any higher, he'd have fallen over backwards.

As if that wasn't intimidating enough, there was the man's face. The skin on it was blotchy and flushed and covered by sideburns that looked like they needed planning permission. The hair on top of his head was a cross between a mane and what you get when you give a two-year-old a crayon. And then there were his eyes.

I don't want to talk about his eyes.

Once he was sure that he had everyone's undivided attention, he started to walk towards us. He took his time. As he passed each teacher they bowed their head as a mark of respect. The sound of his footsteps was the only sound to be heard on the whole yard. It seemed even the wind had decided it had better not ruin his entrance.

By the time the man finally took his place in front of
Hari nobody was in any doubt about what this all meant.

Victory Piggot wasn't going anywhere.

'Did you really think,' he began, 'that I was going
to slink off with my tail between my legs when I
had come so far? You should have seen their faces!'
Victory Piggot indicated the teachers, who didn't even
blink. 'I gave them a moving speech announcing my
retirement and they pretended to feel sorry for me.
We all said how much fun it had been and agreed that
it had been an interesting experiment but, in the long
run, it would probably be in everyone's best interests if
I was to go quietly on my way. Then they drank my
health. Ha!'

Victory Piggot clenched his bony fists and raised them
above his head.

'They got my health all right!' he boomed. 'Isn't it
remarkable how far a little bottle can go when it's
carefully diluted? There was just enough for all of
them to become a little more like me! And as for Mr
Chattersly! Well! As you can see, children, he really has

got my health. In fact, he's got my teeth! He's got my hair! He's got *me*!'

The last three words rang round the yard as Victory Piggot wiped the froth and spittle triumphantly from his moustache. His chest was heaving and his eyes shone. He surveyed his minions and waited for a couple of Second Formers to finish being sick before delivering his final line.

'Now get out of my sight and get to class!'

The rest of the day was a bit of a blur. What was clear was that Hari Patel and Victory Piggot had spun a web of deceit so sticky and dark it could have been made out of Marmite.

Hari had known the truth all along. He had known what Victory Piggot planned to do and he was ready to deal with the fallout.

His first priority was the reporters and how to manage their reports of the morning's events. So they were invited to the gym for a pre-arranged press conference. It lasted over an hour. When they came out, the reporters looked dazed, confused and like none of them had turned down the offer of as much free wine as they could drink. I heard one of them mumbling something into her mobile about Mr Chattersly being 'kept warm and cosy'. Another one was singing about goblins.

There was a glimmer of hope when the police turned up. Some of the teachers' families had seen the TV footage and demanded that the police investigate what Piggot had done to their loved ones.

By 3 p.m. the investigation had curled up and died.

There were two key problems. Firstly, and most importantly, no crime had been committed. When the relatives started giving the inspector a hard time about it, he explained that the last laws to deal with supernatural possession were about five centuries out of date and largely involved drowning witches.

Secondly, whenever the police tried to interview the teachers to get their story, Victory Piggot made them look stupid. He knew that, on the surface, none of the teachers looked any different, so whenever the police or the teachers themselves tried to draw out Victory Pigott's presence within them, he simply refused to show up.

As a result Mr Grieve is now an internet sensation. There's a video of him that's gone viral. He's arguing with himself in the car park after the police have just spoken to him. He's shouting at himself and saying that if he doesn't show himself right now he's going to punch himself so hard he won't know what's hit him. In the end he tries to run himself over, but can't work out the logistics.

Thursday 7th February

This morning Victory Piggot has dedicated himself to letting us know what a real Victorian education feels like.

It hurts.

I have a sore arm, a bruised bum and now my brain hurts as well. If I have one more fact shovelled into my head, I'm pretty sure the whole thing's going to blow.

Every teacher was the same. We were picked on and shouted at. We sat in rows and repeated what they said about a million times. You weren't allowed to talk, you weren't allowed to fidget, and when Danni Grist tried to use her imagination all hell broke loose.

For those who survived, there was lunch. I say 'lunch'. It was a lump of cabbage in a bowl of water. When I'd choked it down I went up to ask if I could have some pudding.

I won't be doing that again.

The afternoon was the longest school afternoon of my life. Literally. We had Piggot himself for chemistry and he wasn't going to let anyone go until we could all repeat the entire periodic table back to him perfectly. We got out at 7 p.m. It would have been 6.30 p.m. but Piggot refused to accept that there were any 'new' elements discovered in the past hundred and fifty years and Sally Coyle just couldn't bring herself to leave them out.

Friday 8th February

Ow.

Saturday 9th February

Just when I thought I'd learned all there is to know about a Victorian education, I found out something new.

They do it at weekends as well.

I think my dad was actually trying to hide how funny

he thought it was when he told me the good news. He didn't try very hard.

Nobody else was laughing when I got to school. The Victory Piggot fan club is now officially dead. Instead the corridors were full of hunched shoulders and shuffling feet. As if the whole thing isn't bad enough, Hari's been working on a poster campaign for next week's visit from the Education Minister. Apparently he's interested in 'Mr Piggot's bold new educational initiative'. The banner above the front entrance says *Nil Sine Labore*, which roughly translated means 'nothing without labour'.

The other banners weren't quite so cheerful.

After lunch, for a 'treat', the whole school had a games afternoon. I was beginning to wonder if it was Victory Piggot's sick idea of a joke when he charged into the boys' changing room dressed for action.

It wasn't a pretty sight.

His shorts were stained and creased. His boots looked like something you used to climb Everest with. But there was something far worse than his boots, his shorts or even his foul-smelling, multi-striped rugby shirt.

His legs.

It was a bit like leaning over the rail of a really tall building. You didn't want to look down but you couldn't help yourself.

It was impossible to work out which bit of his leg was which. He may have had knees and ankles, but masses of curly white hair covered everything. Where you could make out a bit of skin, it was red and angry.

Just like the rest of him.

'Right then, lads! Games!' he said, much too enthusiastically. 'All work and no play makes Jack a dull boy! Eh?' he boomed, slapping Danny Shorey so hard on the back both his contact lenses came out. 'It's just started to rain so I bet you can't wait to start boshing a few bodies and knurling a few heads. Eh? I know I can't.'

A room full of vacant faces stared back at him, although Trevor Neave was starting to look a bit interested.

'We'll play a game of mob football, and just to make it interesting we'll have teachers versus pupils. Hari's volunteered to referee. First team to get the ball onto the crossbar of the opponents' goal wins. You defend the crossbar nearest the school; we defend the one nearest the railway line. Any questions? No? Good. Let's play.'

It didn't take too long to work out the rules of mob football.

There aren't any.

The game started when the ball got flung up high into the air and about one hundred people tried to catch it.

That was the last time I saw it.

The ball disappeared beneath a sea of bodies. I was quite happy to wait for someone to pass it out to me. But when Victory Piggot wasn't trying to get the ball himself, he was walking around the outside of the heap, pushing small people into it and telling them to stop being such big girls' blouses.

Then I got a massive kick up the backside and the next thing I knew I was plunged into a whole world of pain.

It was dark. I couldn't breathe. There was a leg pushing against my throat, but I had no idea whose it was. I was getting pinched and bitten and I think one of the teachers was trying to pull my ear off. I realized I was somewhere in the middle of the heap, but it didn't help. I couldn't work out which way was up and which way was down, let alone plan an escape. It was like a human avalanche. I'd just worked out that I'd been poking myself in the eye with my elbow when all of a sudden I realized I could see daylight again. Somebody had managed to get the ball out of the heap and run away and the rest of the mob was following.

Harry Johnson got about ten metres clear before being mown down by one of Victory Piggot's flying football boots, and another heap soon piled up.

In half an hour the game had moved about fifteen metres.

Then the rain started really hammering down. Within minutes the pitch looked like a battlefield. Every time the heap moved, it took all the grass with it and left behind a muddy, bloody crater. Nobody had the faintest idea who was on which team, and I'm pretty sure we played the last hour without the ball.

When it got so dark you couldn't see anything at all, Victory Piggot eventually blew his whistle.

'Nil-nil!' he boomed, sounding happier than I'd ever heard him. 'Excellent game! Everybody back to the changing rooms for a shower.'

Those who could walk hobbled back to the changing rooms. Those who couldn't, crawled. Those who couldn't do either just stayed where they'd fallen and hoped no one was going to cut the grass for a few days.

As he jogged past me I heard Trevor Neave cheerfully ask Victory Piggot how many games of mob football ended in nil-nil draws.

Apparently they all do.

When I got home my mum asked me who I'd got into a fight with. She thought I was being sarcastic when I said everyone.

Sunday 10th February

This morning the best thing about my life was that it was Sunday.

That lasted until precisely 6.43 a.m. when my dad burst into my room and told me to get changed into my Sunday best because we were going to church. Not content with ruining our school days, Victory Piggot has been telling our parents that he expects them to make sure that 'pupils' home lives are structured, disciplined and reinforce traditional moral standards'.

That's why I look such a prat.

It's also why Mum decided to cook a traditional Sunday lunch.

It wasn't so much a meal as a massacre. Mum couldn't remember what you were supposed to have with roast beef so she cooked it in mint sauce, horseradish and cranberry jelly just to be on the safe side. It was still on fire when Dad wrestled it onto the table. The peas were just about edible but the roast potatoes exploded, the carrots boiled dry and somehow she'd managed to burn the pudding.

It was fruit salad.

If that wasn't bad enough, I was supposed to sit still

and make polite conversation. I'd forgotten just how boring my parents are. After about five minutes I could feel my eyelids surrendering. The next thing I knew, my head hit the table and I got sent to my room for my appalling table manners.

Result.

Monday 11th February

Last night I fell asleep as soon as I'd finished my journal. I'd been planning to spend the rest of the evening trying to work out what to do about Victory Piggot, but it's hard to come up with a cunning plan when you're so tired you can't remember how to clean your own teeth.

School started with the longest assembly ever. There were rules, there was singing, there were more rules, there was kneeling, there was standing, there was much, much more singing and there was asking for forgiveness for what wicked and terrible children we all are.

Just when I thought it couldn't get any worse, the Minister for Education decided to join in.

At first I thought he had something wrong with his eyes. He was peering around the hall like he was

trying to see his audience. I was wondering how come he hadn't noticed the hundreds of bored children in front of him, when I realized he wasn't looking for us at all. He was checking out where the TV cameras were. When he found one, he made sure he smiled right at it.

'I must say, children,' he said to the camera, 'how refreshing it is to see a school assembly that isn't accompanied by the constant shuffling of feet and chewing of gum. And I hope you appreciate how much better you present yourselves because of it.'

The Minister spotted another camera on the other side of the hall and gave it his and-now-I'm-going-to-be-serious face.

'Of course, there is more to school than good behaviour and discipline, but my party believes that a return to these more traditional values is well overdue. We feel that modern society would benefit a great deal from people like you having more structure to your lives and a greater respect for your elders.'

The Minister swung back to the original camera. If he'd bothered to look, he would have noticed that he'd completely lost his audience. Not in the sense that they couldn't follow what he was saying, but because most of them were still trying to work out who he was speaking to.

'I'm going to be around your school all day,' he continued, in a tone of voice that made it sound like a good thing. 'And I hope to see more of the excellent behaviour that has attracted me here in the first place. As you may have heard, we are considering granting the school flagship status, which will mean plenty of money for Mr Piggot and the ambitious plans he has for you.

'However, I don't want to detain you any longer and so, with your permission, Head Master,' the Minister looked at Piggot, who smiled indulgently and gave him a nod, 'class dismissed! I've always wanted to say that.'

Mum and Dad forced me to watch the news when I got home.

'Look! You're on,' Mum said excitedly when the camera showed a close-up of the school's main entrance.

That was about as much of the school as I recognized.

The rest of the filming was in one of the ICT rooms. It's been out of bounds for the past few days. Now I know why. Someone has filled it with fancy pictures, display work that is spelled correctly, and Hari having a 'chat' with the Minister about how much fun computer programming could be and how Mr Piggot had turned round a 'failing culture of pupil-centred learning' at the school.

Even Mum got a bit suspicious.

'I don't think we've met that new teacher, have we?' she asked, as a random pretty woman had a close-up taken of her.

'Neither has anyone else,' I told her. 'She's an actress.'

'Your school's a bit funny sometimes, isn't it?' she said thoughtfully. 'Of course, as long as you're happy there...'

'Me? I'm ecstatic! Who wouldn't want two completely psychotic head teachers in two terms?'

'Well, that's alright then,' she said, taking the dinner plates into the kitchen and once again demonstrating that she couldn't detect sarcasm if it looked her in the face and told her she didn't look a day over twenty-one.

Tuesday 12th February

I couldn't get to sleep last night. The house was still, but my mind was all over the place.

Every time I shut my
eyes, visions of Hari,
Piggot and the Minister
for Education kept
swimming into my head
and pulling faces at me.
The final straw was
Victory Piggot grinning
madly as he put a giant
match to TWW.

That did it.

No one burns my baby.

I got up and pulled out the laptop. There was no time
for a proper paper, but I'd just thought of the next
best thing. The floating faces had given me an idea.

A couple of weeks ago Mr Storey had been trying to
teach us something in ICT. I can't remember what it
was, because I was far more interested in watching
how he reset the starter page for the whole school
network while he thought no one was looking. I had a
feeling it would come in useful.

So, for the past few days, everybody has been logging on to find this 'motivational' message all over their screens:

```
The Child Who Toils Will Never Spoil
```

This morning they booted up to something a little different.

BREAKING NEWS FROM
THE WOODFORD WORD!

THE MINISTER'S A MORON

Education Minister Michael Morrissey took his eye off the ball yesterday in announcing that Woodford School and its mad master, Victory Piggot, should become a 'flagship school'.

My year got sent to the gym after break. I thought we were going there for another assembly, but it was worse than that.

We were going there for gym.

As we arrived Victory Piggot stood in the middle of the room. He was surrounded by wall bars, weights and those weird-looking boxes you're supposed to jump over.

'Good morning, First Years,' he said, clearly replacing the words 'First Years' with 'scum of the earth' in his head as he did so. 'It seems we're left with you. Improbable as it may sound, one of you must be the elusive Jonny Jakes, Fiona Friend or whoever it was who vandalized our electric computer system this morning.

'So, before we all get started would anyone care to step forward and save their fellow pupils from,' Piggot and Hari caught each other's eyes and smiled, 'a rather *vigorous* workout? Any volunteers? No?' Piggot sneered. 'Good. We'll carry on then, shall we?'

At that point a few of the more naturally sadistic teachers came in to join us. They were all wearing shorts and, like Hari, had stopwatches and whistles hanging round their necks. For some reason they were also carrying mops and buckets.

I didn't take it as a good sign.

'Look around you,' Victory Piggot continued once they were all in. 'There are thirty exercise stations around the gymnasium. In a moment you will go to one of them, where you will start that particular exercise. You will be under the close supervision of my colleagues, who will encourage you to do the best you can.'

As he said the word 'encourage', several teachers cracked their knuckles. Victory Piggot waited for the echo to die down.

'After one minute I will blow my whistle and then you will move on to the next station and so on. Any questions?'

Some idiot decided to put his hand up.

'Yes?' Victory Piggot asked.

'Er, when do we stop, sir?' the idiot asked.

Victory Piggot smiled. He walked over to the idiot and bent down. He gently took hold of the idiot's ear and spoke just loudly enough for the rest of us to hear.

'You haven't quite got the hang of all this yet, have you?' he began sweetly. Then his voice began to rise dramatically. 'You start when I tell you to start. You breathe when I tell you to breathe! And you stop when I tell you to stop, which will be when I have found out who Jonny Jakes is! Now get over there and get ready to climb up that rope!'

Piggot blew his whistle in the poor boy's ear. Within seconds the rest of the room divided itself up. The torture was about to begin.

I remember seeing a film about an old war in history class once. There were soldiers trying to run across muddy fields full of barbed wire and there were giant explosions going off all around them. The teacher had asked us to try and imagine what it must have been like. It was difficult at the time.

Now I have an idea.

Within minutes the gym was full of pain. I started off doing push-ups. I'd done twenty when I was 'encouraged' to stop just pushing my bum up and down and keep my body straight.

It stung.

I did five proper push-ups before the whistle went and I was 'encouraged' to climb up and down the wall bars. They were already really sweaty and I slipped and smacked my chin on one.

'Stop bleeding!' Victory Piggot screeched as I wobbled past him on my way to the rope climb.

It didn't go well.

I can't remember much about the other stations. It was all a bit of a blur. There was running involved and jumping and something called a medicine ball that didn't make me feel any better and lots and lots of 'encouragement'. After every minute Piggot would ask for a confession but I was determined not to give up.

At one point
I remember
wondering if Norris
was going to
crack up under the
pressure. I looked
round for him and
saw him giving
Freddy Harris a
piggyback between
some cones while
Mr King threw
tennis balls at him.

He looked like he was enjoying himself.

One agonizing hour later, Piggot blew his whistle for
the last time. Maybe he thought that Jonny Jakes was
just too much of a hero to give up, or maybe he'd just
had enough of the smell. I let out a sigh of relief and
collapsed in a heap.

It was a popular choice.

Norris and I were heading outside after lunch when a whispered voice from behind the recycling bins told me that perhaps the day's torture wasn't yet over.

It was Julie Singh.

'Over here,' she hissed. 'We need to talk.'

'There is no "we",' I protested. 'There stopped being a "we" the moment you wrote for *him*.'

'I'm sorry,' she hissed, still behind the bins. 'Feel better?'

'Yes,' I admitted. I crouched down until I could make out her face. She was wedged tight behind the paper bin and I could see she'd been crying. 'What is it?'

'We've got to do something.'

'About what?'

'What do you think?' Julie stifled a sob. 'About him! And will you just get yourself back here so I don't have to look quite so pathetic!'

'Okay, which particular him?' I asked, once I'd squeezed behind the bin next to Julie.

'Both of them. Piggot's bad enough, but now Hari's become a monster too.'

'He won't take no for an answer,' another familiar voice piped up from behind the glass recycling skip. 'He's forcing us to be part of his propaganda machine,' Sally moaned.

'What's a propaganda machine?' Norris wanted to know as he squeezed in next to me.

'He wants us to write anything he tells us to,' Julie explained.

'Or what?' I asked.

'Or we're the first.' Sally's voice was thin and shaky. She looked terrified.

'The first what?' Norris said.

'The first to be tested,' Sally stammered. 'Mr Piggot

wants to start his old experiments up again. If we
don't do what Hari asks, we're going to be the first
guinea pigs.'

'So what are you going to do?' I wanted to know.

'I don't know, do I!' Julie snapped. 'That's why I'm
asking for your help behind a recycling bin! I've said
I'm sorry, what more do you...'

Suddenly the wheelie bin me and Norris were crouched
behind was rattled away. In its place appeared Victory
Piggot and his right-hand man.

'These two?' Hari asked Piggot in a disdainful tone, pointing at us. 'Are you sure they're what you're after, Head Master? They're fairly pathetic specimens.'

'I'm sure,' Piggot growled. 'They were in Chattersly's office the day I arrived. They were never properly punished then, so I see no reason for them not to give something back to the school now.'

'As you wish, Head Master. These two,' Hari commanded. The two lab technicians who had rolled the wheelie bin away came forward, grabbed us by the elbows and marched us into the school building. Hari and Piggot fell in behind us.

I looked over my shoulder. Julie was clutching her mouth in shock. For a split second I wondered if we'd just been set up, but then I remembered that she couldn't act for toffee. It was one of her more attractive personality traits.

As we were led across the playground, no one looked remotely surprised to see a couple of Year Sevens being dragged along the corridor by Piggot's lackeys. I had the technician with the purple hair.

Her nails were digging into my skin.

'That hurts,' I told her. 'You don't have to pinch me!'

Piggot whacked the back of my head.

'Keep a civil tongue in your head, boy.'

'But ... where are you taking us?' I spluttered. Stars swam in front of my eyes and fear cartwheeled round my guts as the prospect of Piggot's experiments suddenly took an unwanted grip on my imagination. 'You can't just...'

This time it was Hari who cuffed the other side of my head.

'Mr Piggot can just do whatever he sees fit in order to maintain the smooth running of the school,' he said.

More stars started to dance in front of me. The grip on my elbow tightened as we headed for the stairs. I had a horrible feeling I knew where we were going.

Sure enough we soon found ourselves in the gloomy

corridor leading to Piggot's old office. He had fitted it out with some old-fashioned lamps, but it was still cold and full of shadows.

It suited him.

I was surprised when we halted. Instead of Piggot's old office, we had stopped outside another door. It was protected with three different padlocks.

'Inside,' Piggot instructed us once Hari had undone the locks.

'No,' resisted Norris. It was a brave move.

But foolish.

The lab technician with the tattoos struck him a harsh blow to the kidneys and he was dragged, groaning, into a leather chair and strapped down.

I got shoved into one next to him.

We were in what was unmistakably a laboratory. There were test tubes, Bunsen burners, clamps and frothing bottles of liquid. Amongst other things I was starting to seriously regret not going to the toilet earlier.

'Now then, boys, there's no need to be alarmed,' Piggot began, in a softer voice than usual. 'We're not going to particularly harm you.'

It was the least reassuring thing anyone has ever said to me.

'I just need to ensure that the breakthrough research I began is not lost,' Piggot continued. The anger in his face had gone. It was a shame it had to be replaced by the crazy stare of a mad scientist. 'You understand, don't you?'

I could tell it was a rhetorical question by the way the lab technicians were putting gags in our mouths.

'Don't worry about those,' Piggot said. 'They're just for your protection. Stop you biting your tongues off. Ready?'

'Ready, sir,' Hari's voice sounded behind me. He was staring at me. Weirdly. It was like he'd just seen me properly for the first time. 'But can I just ask this boy a few questions?'

'Another time, Hari!' Piggot snapped. 'Science first. Questions later. Now, who shall we begin with?'

My arms were firmly strapped down, so I jerked my head in Norris' direction. Unfortunately Piggot mistook it for a nod.

'Good lad!' he boomed. 'Take one for the team, eh? Now then, this won't hurt too much.'

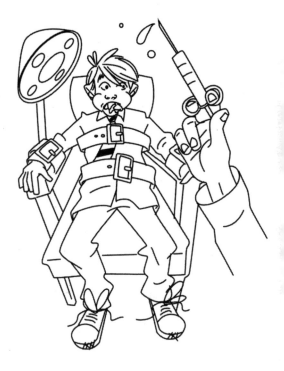

I closed my eyes. It wasn't like I needed to actually see the gigantic needle heading for a well-padded part of my body. I felt a sharp sting in the top of my left arm, followed by a strong, dull ache.

'That's it. Not too bad, was it?' Piggot said, bizarrely

cheerful. 'Sit tight while we sort your friend out. Then one more little stab and we'll be done.'

I kept my eyes shut and tried not to imagine what Piggot was up to. He hadn't done an experiment for over a century. Just because he wasn't trying to deliberately hurt us didn't mean he wasn't accidentally going to kill us.

A second jab went into my left arm. It was sore already and I yelled in pain. I could feel the warm ooze of something being pumped in. I felt faint. My head was on fire and everything was spinning. Before I knew it, I'd puked all over my lap.

'Euurrgh!' Hari yelled. He'd been in the firing line too and was covered in globules of vomit. Piggot wasn't best pleased either.

'Subject one unsuitable!' he shouted at the lab technicians. He tugged his moustache and creased his forehead. 'Unable to retain active ingredient.'

One lab technician took a note. The second injected Norris. Piggot watched nervously. A minute and no puking later, he cheered up again.

'Subject two suitable!' he crowed, 'and to be detained for observation for ninety minutes.' He smiled and patted Norris on the shoulder as if he was a pet. Then his expression darkened as he made his way back to my chair.

'Your friend, however, is going to leave us. This of course is on the understanding that if he mentions what has happened here to anyone. And I mean anyone!' He glared at me. Hari hadn't stopped glaring at me. 'Then I will dedicate the rest of my time on this earth to finding a particularly unpleasant active ingredient that he can digest. *Permanently.*'

'Head Master, before he goes could I just...'

'Not now, Hari,' Piggot interrupted angrily. 'I want this ... inferior specimen out of my way. Immediately. I am not interested in failure.'

I tried to stare Piggot out to show I hadn't taken his insults personally, but his eyes were bulging with manic energy so I gave up. Behind him, Norris was angrier than I'd ever seen him. His wrists were straining against the leather straps and a vein in his neck was pulsing dangerously. He was giving Piggot the sort of stare that made anyone who wanted to tackle him on the rugby pitch suddenly realize their bootlaces were undone.

On Piggot's signal the lab technicians undid my straps. Hari was literally biting his lip in order to avoid upsetting his master further. I racked my brains to try and work out why he'd started to suspect me. Had he seen me in the corridor back when we found the diary? Had I done my English homework too well again and blown him away with my literary genius?

As I got up, I tried to give Norris a sign that I wouldn't rest until I'd defeated the forces of darkness.

It was a shame it sprayed some of my sick over him.

I stumbled up to the main corridor. Images of Norris, strapped down and struggling, were racing round my head. The remaining contents of my stomach weren't exactly playing it cool either. I held on to a doorway for support.

I made it to the toilets, pulled my jumper off and threw it straight in the bin. Then I splashed some water on my face and began to feel a little more human. I checked myself in the mirror, looking into my eyes for answers.

Did I still have what it took to defeat the forces of darkness?

Tick.

Even when they stuck big needles into people?

There was a longer pause.

Tick.

Relieved, I headed out again. I suppose I was going home, but I couldn't be sure. My brain had decided to let my feet make their own decisions while it tried to figure out how to free Norris from Piggot's clutches.

I got as far as the next corner before a pair of hands grabbed me and pulled me into the Drop In Zone. The same hands pushed me onto the bean bags.

'I wonder how much they'd give me?' Michelle Bell's face leered over me. 'What do you think you're worth?'

I tried to collect my thoughts. It wasn't easy with the room spinning round so quickly.

'Er, what?'

'You. Squirt. I reckon you could make me a lot richer.'

'Er, what?' I wondered again. I was struggling to access the rest of my vocabulary.

'Although I suppose I'd have to prove it somehow,' Michelle grinned, her hands on her hips. 'I mean, you're not much to look at, are you? That's why it took me so long!'

She reached into the inside pocket of her blazer. It was her turn to show me some pictures.

'Of course, I could use the picture I took of you raiding Mr Chattersly's competition box. Or perhaps the sneaky snapshot I took of you filling the lockers with *The Woodford Word* last week.'

I tried to think of something to rescue me, but nothing came. On top of everything else, Michelle Bell had beaten me at my own game. She bent down to grab my wrists.

'Easy, tiger!' she said as I lashed out. 'I'm pulling you up, not taking you prisoner, you wally.'

'What?'

Michelle laughed. 'It's your lucky day, *Jonny.* I've decided you're worth more on the loose than you are in whatever dungeon Piggot's got lined up for you. I've just seen Hari: he was running up from the basement calling your name. Your real name. Lucky everyone else has gone home, isn't it? I think he's starting to work it out, too.'

'But how...'

'Put him down!'

Michelle Bell let go of my hand and turned to see Julie and Sally advancing cautiously towards her. She assessed the situation.

'Or you're going to hit me with two rolls of A3 paper?'

Julie tried not to look embarrassed. 'If we have to!'

'OMG!' Michelle squawked suddenly. 'It's all of you, isn't it? *The Woodford Word*. Ankle-biters united!' While she was distracted I reached down to see if my fingers could find something better for an improvised weapon.

They didn't.

'Jonny, if anything, a bean bag is even less terrifying. Alright! Enough!' Michelle's smile vanished as we continued to threaten her with stationery and soft furnishings. 'I'm not here to grass you up, Jonny. I'm here,' she sighed, 'to save you.'

Sally and Julie halted their advance. 'Oh,' Sally said, confused. 'That's what we were doing.'

'Well, give me a hand then. Hari's suspicious,' Michelle explained again. 'Him and that lab technician with the weird hair are running around looking for you.'

'So we need to get you out of here,' Julie summarized. 'What about Norris?'

I shook my head. 'Piggot said he'd let him go in a bit. He's still down there.'

'You don't look so good,' Sally sympathized. 'Can I get you anything?'

'No time,' Julie cut in, looking out of the window. 'The lab tech's heading this way. We need a disguise.'

We looked around. The Drop In Zone was big on cushions, but it didn't have much to offer on the disguise front. Unfortunately Michelle Bell then realized she had a make-up bag.

'No way!' I protested as she shook it at me.

'You haven't got a choice,' Michelle grinned, pulling out a metal tube and revealing a hideous pink lipstick.

'And we're going to have to be quick!' Julie commanded.

The girls stared at me. I stared straight back. If I was going to become a girl, they'd have to make me.

It turns out Michelle Bell is very good at that sort of thing.

Three minutes later I was ready. We didn't get far.

'Where are you going?' the tattooed lab assistant demanded.

'Home,' Michelle replied, gripping me hard by the arm to prevent me wiping off my eyeshadow.

'Have you seen a boy?'

We shook our heads.

'What's with all the make-up?' the lab assistant wanted to know, pulling her face close to mine. I looked down and fiddled with my skirt.

I hope to never repeat that sentence again.

'She's just been dumped,' Michelle replied for me. 'She doesn't want her boyfriend to know she's been crying.' The lab technician kept her face inches from mine, examining my 'boyfriend' misery. Satisfied, she let out a harsh laugh.

'Welcome to the real world!' she jeered, then lost interest. She headed back along the corridor. We ran off in the other direction.

I hoped it would have a massive hole in the ground.

'Thanks,' I gasped when we'd made it beyond the school gates. I wiped my forehead. My hand became instantly covered in make-up. 'I think.'

'Any time,' Michelle grinned. 'Maybe next time you can be a blonde?'

Sally tried not to laugh. Julie was less successful.

'Okay, so I'm going to go home now and you're going to do all that saving-the-day-in-secret stuff. Just remember you can call me if you need me,' Michelle continued, starting to head off. 'Laters, losers.'

I wasn't sure what to say so I waved. The girls joined in.

'Right,' I said when she'd gone. 'Priority one: shower. Priority two: meet you at Norris' house later.'

'If he gets out,' Sally worried.

'Heh, I saw the look on his face when I left,' I assured

her. 'Trust me. He's getting out.'

Once we'd gone our separate ways, I ran all the way home. Unnatural, but it had its advantages. I got home before my parents and was seen by as few people as possible.

As I burst through the door, the phone rang.

'Yeah?' I panted, out of breath. There was a pause. I could feel confusion on the other end of the line.

'Hello, could I speak to your mum or dad please?'

The sweat froze on my forehead.

It was Hari.

He was trying to put on a fake voice, but I'd have recognized it anywhere. I calculated swiftly: he'd paused because he'd been unsure; the panting had masked my voice; he'd asked for my parents to be on the safe side; I was better than Hari at fake voices.

'That would be difficult!' I blustered, doing my best to sound like my dad as I deliberately kept up the panting. 'Bearing in mind they live in Sunderland. Look, who is it and what is it? I've just got back from my run and I need a shower.'

Hari bought it, but all I'd bought was a little time. He said I needed to bring my son in for an urgent meeting with the Head Master, and I agreed. But when I didn't get frogmarched to school within half an hour, he was going to know he'd been tricked. It was time to disappear.

Priority one was going to have to wait.

Ten minutes later I was crawling through Norris' bedroom window and flopping onto his floor. I'd left a note on my door explaining to my parents that I was running away, but for them not to feel bad, because it wasn't their fault. Just to buy more time, I 'accidentally' left the train times to Scunthorpe scribbled on a note by my bed.

A muffled voice came from the region of the bed. To my relief, Norris had made it home.

Scunthorpe nice this time of year? Departure times: 17:35 18:16 18:47

Scunthorpe run away paradise

'Go away. I'm not hungry.'

'Norris,' I whispered. 'It's me. What happened?'

The duvet rustled. Norris poked his face above it.

'I don't know how you live like this,' Norris replied gloomily. 'Why do you look like a girl?'

'Live like what?' I asked, keen to steer the conversation back to the original question.

'With this,' he said, pointing to his stomach.

'Eh?'

'With this,' he said, pointing to his stomach again. 'It doesn't do anything!'

'I'm not getting "this",' I explained. 'What did Piggot inject you with? Did he pass on something from me?'

'He gave me your appetite,' Norris groaned. 'He probably tried to give you mine. You know, like the wren and the spider in Jennings' diary? It's terrible. How can someone only like three types of food?'

'What other types are there?'

Norris groaned again.

'Hari knows my secret identity,' I told him, hoping the news would snap him out of it. 'He thinks my dad is about to bring me into school. It's a nightmare: I can't go to school, I can't go home, I...'

'Slow down,' Norris complained. 'Think it through. And maybe take a shower while you do it,' he added, wrinkling his nose.

Norris helped me sneak to the bathroom. I was a

190

lot happier with my appearance when I came out.
Norris was much happier with the aroma. I was also
surprisingly pleased to see the girls at Norris' window.

'Norris!' Julie said with a sigh of relief as she slithered
in. Sally's face followed behind. She looked ashamed.

'Did it hurt?'

'A bit,' Norris patted his stomach awkwardly. 'It could
have been worse.'

'It should have been me,' Julie said apologetically.

'And me,' Sally agreed.

'Erm, no! Technically I think you'll find it shouldn't
have been anyone!' I interrupted. 'And perhaps we
should stop feeling quite so sorry for ourselves and
work out what we're going to do about it?' I punched
the bed for emphasis. 'We need to get back into that
lab.'

'No!' Norris protested.

'Why?' asked Sally.

'Proof.' Julie took the word from my mouth. Then she added some more of her own. 'Documents, pictures of what he's up to. Plus we have to stop what he's doing. He's managed to change Norris' appetite: what's he going to do next?'

'I am not being turned into anything else!' I said with feeling.

'I've just had a horrible thought,' Sally muttered. I could see that she was trying to keep control of the contents of her stomach.

'What is it?'

'What if he wants everyone to turn into him?'

'It's already happening,' Norris agreed after a heavy silence. 'Haven't you noticed the teachers? He's not just in their heads any more. He's spreading.'

I nodded. Norris was right. It was subtle, but it was there in the little things. The teachers were marching more than they were walking, their hands were gradually tightening into fists, and their voices were becoming deeper.

Julie could see it too. 'We have to act tonight then. Now.'

'And do what?' Sally wanted to know.

'The laboratory,' Julie answered her. 'We have to stop Piggot's work. Destroy it. In fact, what are we waiting for?'

I held up my hand. 'Too soon. They'll be expecting something.'

'And they'll be awake,' Norris agreed. We caught each other's eye. We both knew where we were going next with this. At our last sleepover, we'd been looking at a website about the world's secret police. It had some handy tips.

'Four a.m.,' I began.

'Universally recognized and proven to be the best time

for a raid,' Norris continued, quoting from Ultimate Soldier.

'Targets are fatigued.'

'They lose control of higher functions.'

'And are psychologically compromised in 78% of all...'

'Enough of the boy talk,' Julie hissed. 'I get it. What are we going to do until then?'

Norris tapped his nose and caught my eye again. 'Use the Ultimate Soldier's best secret weapon.'

'Which is?' Julie sighed.

'Sleep,' we said together smugly.

And to think my mum believes that the internet rots your brain.

4 a.m. February 13th. Masked figures break in to a secret underground laboratory. Their mission: to save mankind.

Again.

I am *so* getting a film done of my life.

Julie had already pocketed her mum's school keys, so the main entrance was no problem. My lock-picking kit put paid to the padlocks on the lab door.

A science laboratory is a home from home for Sally, so she quickly put us to work. She told me and Norris what to photograph while she and Julie raided the filing cabinets.

'So now we destroy it?' I asked when we had gathered the proof we needed.

'I guess.' Sally shrugged. You could tell that the idea of undoing years of ground-breaking research wasn't going down easily.

'Suits me!' Norris said with considerably more enthusiasm. He grabbed a bottle with *mercaptoacetic acid* on the label. 'I think I'm getting my appetite back and I'm *not* going through that again.'

'Watch out!' Sally warned as Norris raised his arm to smash the bottle on the floor.

It was too late.

A vile smell exploded out of the broken bottle. About three seconds later, the contents of our stomachs exploded into the sinks.

'Better out than in,' Norris consoled us once we could all breathe again. 'I guess I didn't have anything left to be sick with.'

'What was *that*?' Julie wanted to know, tears streaming from her eyes.

'It's a volatile compound rich in sulphur,' Sally explained with her hand still hovering by her mouth.

'It stinks!' I complained, wiping my mouth. Then I stopped mid-wipe.

My stomach was still cramping and my head was swimming, but something new was trying to say hello. I held a finger to my lips for silence.

'What is it?' Julie whispered, her thoughts immediately turning to the door and the corridor beyond.

'Shhh,' I insisted. 'I'm trying to think. Somebody said something. Us. Just now. I think it's important. Sally, what did you just say?'

'Er ... it's a volatile compound.'

'It wasn't that. Julie?'

'What was that?'

'No. Norris?'

Norris puffed out his cheeks in the effort to remember.
'You were being sick,' he thought aloud. 'What do you
say when someone's being sick?'

'Yuck?' I guessed.

Norris shook his head. 'It was something else.'

Sally shut her eyes and tried to replay the conversation
in her head. 'Better out than in,' she said triumphantly a
few moments later.

'And he said he had nothing left in his stomach because
of his appetite,' Julie added, pointing at Norris.

At last my thought paddled its way to the surface.

'That's it! All this,' I indicated the camera, the
documents we'd stolen and the broken glass on the floor.
'That doesn't put an end to it. It's in here,' I tapped
my head. 'In his head. He'll work it out again. It's *him*
we need to get rid of.'

'But what about the teachers?' Julie queried. 'He's infected all of them. Do we have to get rid of them as well?'

'It's a nice idea,' I agreed. 'But it's only what's *in* them that's the problem,' I explained. 'We don't have to get rid of them, as long as we can get Piggot out of them.'

'And how do we do that?' Julie wanted to know.

I looked around the lab, at all the mysterious potions left on the shelves. I visualized and then I grinned.

'By making science a whole lot more fun.'

We crept into Norris' garage at 5.30 a.m. and gently dumped our rucksacks before turning on the light. We'd taken what we needed from the lab and relieved the Duke of Edinburgh store of a few essential items.

Norris peered cautiously outside as the rest of us took in the hulks of dismantled engines spread out around us. Tools lined the walls and two steel trolleys were crammed full of more. It looked like Norris' dad knew his way round a spanner.

'We're okay,' Norris assured us as he came back in. 'No lights in the house and the street's empty.'

'First things first, then,' Sally instructed. 'Everyone grab a mask.'

We pulled on the masks and got to work. Norris was in charge of engineering. Sally did the chemistry. Me and Julie did what we were told.

An hour of dangerous and foul-smelling work later, we were ready for the next phase.

Norris and I pulled the rucksacks back on and headed off to school. Julie and Sally went to organize backup and make an appearance at breakfast.

I made it, undetected, to break time. Or, as Victory Piggot has decided to rename it, Whole School Singing Practice. Apparently it was going to be an experience that united us in our 'core values' while providing 'hearty exercise' and 'joyous fellowship'.

I can confidently report that the pupils had a different way of describing it.

The 'joyous fellowship' bit definitely looked in short supply as everyone tried to squeeze their bottoms onto the cold floor, although you could argue that there was some 'hearty exercise' between the hard kids and anyone else who tried to sit near them.

When the children were seated, the teachers handed out the hymn books before taking their places on the stage above in comfy chairs.

Presumably the teachers' 'core values' translated into sitting as far away from the pupils as possible.

'Hymn five hundred and sixty-one: "Rise from your graves, ye dead",' Piggot commanded, forcing everyone back to their feet again. 'But, before we begin, I am sure you are aware that there are a couple of whole-school matters we need to address.'

Piggot stalked to the front of the stage. His eyebrows lowered and his eyes glinted below them like diamonds stuck in a thorn bush.

'On the plus side,' he began, in a voice that could trigger avalanches. 'The Minister for Education has decided to make our school a flagship school! That means that what goes on at Woodford School will provide a basis for improvement for the rest of the country!

'Just think,' he pounded the lectern, 'soon the whole of Britain will once again be back on the path to greatness! Punishment will pave the way and discipline will no longer be a dirty word!

'However!' he shrieked, hitting the top of his crescendo. 'First there is the matter of our snake in the grass. Our toad in the hole. The one who wants to ruin it for everyone: Jonny Jakes.'

I looked across at Norris. He wondered if that should be our signal. I shook my head.

'And now,' Piggot continued. 'Thanks to Hari, we are going to flush the viper from its nest.'

Norris looked again. I shook my head again. I wanted to know what animal I was going to be next.

And besides, timing was everything.

'That's right, Head Master,' Hari piped up from below. 'Boys and girls. Fellow pupils. I am sure that you, like me, have often wondered who Jonny Jakes really is. Well, yesterday, I finally worked it out.'

Hari soaked up the attention of the hall and spun out his moment of triumph.

'And today, now, we will put an end to his campaign of fear and mistruth. In a few seconds, with the press of a button, his face will appear on this projector screen. Just before I do that, however, we want you to know two things. The first is that the reward for handing Jonny Jakes to us is one thousand pounds.'

A murmuring filled the room.

A slightly more enthusiastic murmuring than I would
have liked.

Norris looked across again. I nodded and held my hand
up, ready to count down from five on my fingers.

Julie, Sally and Michelle began to move stealthily
through the crowd of pupils to take up their positions.

Five.

Hari carried on, oblivious to the two heavily armed
figures hanging amongst the lighting bars and scenery
above him. 'The second thing you need to know is that
no one...'

Four.

'...is leaving here until he is handed over...'

Three.

'...or we are told exactly where we can find him.'

Two.

'Good.' Hari appreciated the stony silence. 'I'm glad that's understood.'

One.

'So, let's do this.'

Zero.

My hand became a fist. It was showtime.

Hari went for the remote control, but before he got there, he was plunged into darkness. Julie had killed the lights above the stage and, at the same instant, Sally had rattled the red curtain across the front of it.

A second later, six pairs of rubber gloves full of butyric acid sank softly through the darkness towards the bewildered teachers below. I could hear the squelch as they hit the floor. I was glad I had a mask on to protect me from what happened next.

Sally was right. If you want to make people sick, then a very good place to start is with the smell of sick.

The rotten eggs we'd got from the food bins went next in four more rubber gloves. This time even the mask couldn't completely block out the smell. It had been a touch of genius to mix them with the milk.

Especially when you think just how out of date it was.

Happy that we had got things successfully under way, me and Norris switched on our head torches. I was treated to a spectacular aerial view of Mr Chang. He was clutching his throat and stumbling around in his own sick.

Looking around, it seemed a standard manoeuvre.

We abseiled down. One hand controlled the descender, and the other one got busy on the trigger handle of the spray bottles we'd unhooked from our utility belts. It was time for trimethylamine to join the party. You could tell Sally had formulated it perfectly by the way the varnish on the stage's wooden floor started peeling.

With our feet dangling above the heads of the stricken teachers, me and Norris arrested our descents and swung the straps round on our backs. Taking care to fire away from each other, we put Norris' improvised puke pumps to work. The putrescine cocktail shot out.

So did more sick.

When we finally hit the stage and unclipped, a few teachers tried to come after us. In the criss-cross of our torch beams it was a bit like a zombie movie where they all close in on you. Really slowly. One of them, with his hand over his mouth, got hold of my mask, but just as he was about to try and pull it off, Norris managed to uncork something very unpleasant right under his nose. All of a sudden my attacker had other matters that needed his attention.

It's amazing how fast people can think when they're desperate. Another teacher had put a cushion cover over his head to protect him from the stench. It was working enough for him to be making steady progress towards where he thought the fire exit was.

I reached down for the glass vial tucked into my sock and thrust it up under the cushion cover. Then I crushed it in my gloved hand. A warm red ooze trickled over my wrist. Followed by a green torrent of stomach juice.

The teacher sank to his knees.

It felt cruel to keep going, but the plan was only going to work if we did it properly. 'Better out than in' meant we couldn't leave anything behind. If we'd learned anything about Victory Piggot, it was that he wasn't leaving unless he absolutely had to.

Somewhere in the background I could hear that the pupil evacuation process on the other side of the curtains was in its final stages. It was a good job. The curtains were starting to curl up and die, just like everyone else wanted to do behind them.

Eventually our supplies were exhausted and I was as keen as the teachers to get out. The rubber on the mask was starting to perish and the hideous stink was trying to creep in. We waited as long as we could as teacher after teacher heaved and retched until nothing more seemed to be coming out. Then I stuck my hand through the curtains and waved.

The lights above the stage came back on and the three masked girls ran in to join us. We gave each other the thumbs up.

Each of the girls was carrying two large funnel-shaped devices strapped to their back. They looked like cosmic ray guns but they were better than that.

They were hairdryers.

Big hairdryers.

A tidal wave of hot air began to roll around the stage.

A few seconds later a foul mist of vomit vapour started to drift up from the floor. Soon the mist had become a fog and I couldn't see a thing. I kept wiping my eyes, but it didn't help.

I was getting panicky with the smell and the heat and the sense that something was wrong. It felt like I was going to suffocate. Climbing over the moaning bodies, I eventually made it to the fire exit and shoved it open. The fog wobbled and then decided it needed some air.

It wasn't the only one.

In a few seconds there was a full-on gale as fresh air flooded in and the fog flew out.

The stage was full of pale-faced teachers clutching their stomachs and begging for water. We couldn't risk it, though. Who knew, maybe somewhere in the mist, the faintest trace of Victory Piggot was still alive and all it needed was one contaminated drink and we'd be back where we started.

I pointed at the door and mimed crawling outside. They got the message. Soon there was a long line of teachers crawling towards the playground. Their tongues were hanging out and their eyeballs were bursting.

I couldn't resist taking a picture.

Out in the open a few of the teachers felt up to asking questions. 'What's going on?' was pretty popular, followed by 'Why do I smell so much?', 'Why have I got sweet corn in my hair?' and, finally, 'Has he gone?'

I spun round. The nagging sense of something being

wrong had just turned into a big fat throbbing reality.

'Where's Piggot?' I yelled at the others. 'Or Chattersly?'

Michelle Bell pulled her mask off for a better view.

'Not here,' she shook her head.

'When did you last see him?' Julie asked.

'And what about Hari?' Sally wondered.

'Nooo!' I stamped the ground in frustration.

'Owww!' Miss Frustup yelped. I'd just stepped on her outstretched finger. 'That way,' she said hoarsely. 'Both of them. Wrapped up in his gown.'

'Where do you think he's taking him?' Sally asked as we ran off in the direction of Miss Frustup's crumpled finger.

'The lab,' I panted. 'Got to be. Come on!'

'Wait,' Michelle Bell demanded. 'There's no point going in the main door.'

'I can pick the locks,' I pointed out.

'He'll be ready for you, though. I know another way.'

Instead of the main building, Michelle led us out to the playground. Specifically the bit of it behind the recycling bins, where we'd met Julie and Sally the day before.

'Look. Here.' Michelle pointed to an iron grille set into the tarmac. Then she lay down on her stomach and put her ear up to it. 'Listen.'

We fanned out around the grille on our stomachs, our ears close to the bars.

'There, there,' a voice drifted up to us. It was Piggot's, but even weirder than normal. It sounded as if he was trying to comfort a baby. 'Just think what we can do, Hari. Together. Forever.'

I felt dizzy. The pages of Robert Jennings' diary were suddenly swimming in front of my eyes.

'Haven't I done enough, Head Master?' a second voice floated up. It was terrified, just like another schoolboy had been over a hundred years ago.

'You have served me well, Hari,' Piggot explained patiently. 'And soon you shall serve me further. Forever! And then Hari, then the world is ours.'

'Put your torch on,' Michelle whispered. 'See. There's a door, down there. I bet he doesn't even know it's there.'

We peered through the grate in the torchlight. Sure enough, there was an old door with a small vent at the top through which we'd heard the voices.

'Probably had steps down to it years ago,' Michelle explained. 'They've walled them up, though. Give me a hand, Norris.'

'Have you got your stuff for the lock?' Julie asked as Norris and Michelle heaved the grille out of the way.

'Always be prepared,' I nodded. 'Okay, lower me down.'

Four sets of hands began to feed me through the new hole in the playground. It was narrow and seemed to get narrower the further I dropped into it. By the time my feet were on the floor, I was already pressed up against the door.

I looked at the lock. It was an old-fashioned five-lever mortice lock. I had just the thing. There was only one problem.

I couldn't reach it.

No matter how I squirmed, I couldn't get my hand to the pouch hanging on the back of my utility belt. I wasn't exactly stuck, but every time I tried to reach behind me, my elbow had an argument with the narrow walls. And every time the walls won.

'*Your youth,*' Piggot's manic voice floated through the vent again, '*my brains. Our ambition. Just think about it!*'

'*I don't want to think about it!*' Hari squealed. '*I wish I'd never even heard of you. You're mad!*'

'What are you doing?' Julie was leaning into the hole. 'We haven't got long.'

'I can't move,' I explained. 'It's too narrow.'

'Put me down, then. I'm smaller than you.'

'But you don't know how to pick a lock.'

'*You're nervous. I understand, Hari,*' Piggot soothed. '*But there's nothing to worry about. Just imagine: immortality.*'

'Well, it looks like I'm going to have to learn real fast. Come on!'

Four sets of hands lifted me out again.

'Okay,' I said as I handed over my tools to Julie. 'This is the bolt retractor. This is the lever lifter. With this one you're lifting a lever that is holding the bolt locked. This one twists and pushes the bolt back. Got it?'

'Lift the lever, retract the bolt. Simple,' Julie nodded as I mimed the actions again.

'And Julie?'

'Yeah?'

'I know it doesn't feel like the right occasion for it, but don't rush. If you...'

'*Nearly there,*' Piggot's voice interrupted again, as manic as ever. '*This tube goes in here, this tube goes in here, I press this and then we sit tight.*'

'*Helllllp!*'

'Are you sure about that?' Julie wanted to know.

'Seriously!' I grabbed her shoulders. 'If you lose the picture of the lock in your head, you could be trying for hours.'

'Sure,' Julie nodded, understanding. 'Let's go.'

When Julie was on the ground I leaned in as far as I dared. I focused my torch beam on the lock and kept talking in the calmest voice I could manage.

'Angle it up. Good. Find the tension. Don't rush. If it feels wrong, try again, no big deal.'

'I don't want to work for you any more! Let me go!'

Hari pleaded desperately, his voice frail and high.

'What's a little pain when you've got the rest of a long life to forget it?' Piggot's voice sounded woozy, almost as if he were drunk. 'Maybe we can sing something together. Take your mind off it?'

Hari whimpered something unintelligible. Then I heard a wonderful sound.

Click.

'Got it!' Julie yelled.

'Who's that?' Hari yelled, coming back to life. 'I'm in here! Help!'

'Relax, Hari,' Piggot's voice was wavering more and more. 'Everything's going to be alright. God save our gracious Queen ... God save...'

'It's okay, Hari! We're coming!' Julie grabbed the handle and pushed at the door. It gave an inch but no further.

'You're going to have to kick it or something,' Sally

explained. 'It's probably got a cupboard or shelves in front of it.'

'Shelves!' Julie said five seconds later as her second kick did the trick. I made a mental note to ask her later how the heck she generated so much power in so little space. Now didn't seem the appropriate time.

'Okay, put me down again!' I told the others.

With the door half open, I helped Julie kick and barge the rest of her way into Piggot's lab. When we'd finished, there was dust, glass and splinters everywhere.

As the debris settled, two hospital-type beds came into focus. So did the figures on them: Hari and Piggot. Hari was strapped down to his bed; a pale and weakened Piggot was writhing on the one next to him.

'Soon. Soon,' Piggot muttered. His eyeballs rolled back in his head.

'Help me!' Hari begged.

'This tube!' Julie drew my attention away to one long

winding tube amongst many. One end snaked to Piggot's forearm, the other to Hari's. I tried not to look at the needles. 'What's that?' Julie pointed to a dark fluid. It was making its way slowly from Piggot's end of the tube to Hari's.

'Well,' I said, pinching the tube between Hari and the leading edge of the dark fluid. 'I don't know the technical term for it, but for our purposes I reckon we can call it Piggot sauce.'

'What are you doing?' Hari wailed, looking at my fingers on the tube.

'Just what I wanted to know,' Julie seconded. 'Don't worry about pinching it. Just get it out of his arm!'

'I don't like needles,' I explained, keeping my grip. 'And here's some other things I don't like, Hari: rival newspapers, people who suck up to authority and, most of all, anyone who threatens to reveal my secret identity!'

'I won't, I promise!' Hari pleaded. 'Just get me out of here.'

'But how can I trust you?' I demanded, my fingers still gripping the tube.

'Because sometimes you just have to!' Julie answered for him. 'Like me. Trusting me.'

'And me,' Sally agreed, making her entrance.

'Yup. Me too,' Norris chipped in, dusting himself off. 'We're on your side, remember. Just take it out, mate.'

I looked at my team. I looked down at the terrified face of my bitter rival.

For some reason it didn't feel as good as it should have done.

I grimaced and pulled the needle out of Hari's arm.

'In here.' Julie came over to me with an empty bottle. She put Hari's end of the tube into it. 'And this time it doesn't get locked in a cupboard. Agreed?'

I released my grip on the tube. The fluid made its way to the bottle. 'Agreed.'

We watched the last of Piggot's essence drain into the small bottle.

'Thanks,' Hari said as we undid the straps on his wrists. 'I mean it. I was wrong.'

'Bit of an understatement,' I suggested, but a groan from the other bed prevented me from going into further detail.

'Are you alright, sir?' Sally was bent over Mr Chattersly. He was looking pale and confused. 'It's okay, sir. He's gone! Back in his bottle. The one that's just being stamped on by those boys.'

Mr Chattersly blinked and looked around him. 'But where am I? Where's he gone? What ... happened?'

'Don't worry,' Norris smiled and patted Hari on the back. 'Hari's going to explain it to you. Every last word.'

'Hari?' Chattersly pushed the name around feebly. He looked like a baby trying to remember what a spoon did again. I reached for my camera, but Julie made me put it back in my pocket.

'Who's Hari?' Chattersly wanted to know, his memory still struggling. 'And who are you? What's your name?' he muttered, turning to face me. His eyes were still rapidly going in and out of focus.

'Oh, don't worry about that, sir,' I said cheerfully as we all headed back out to Michelle, who was offering us a hand up. 'It's really not important.'

TOP SECRET

Author Malcolm Judge lives in a large Cumbrian village with his wife and three sons. When he's not teaching drama, he enjoys cycling and refereeing at the local rugby club. Besides writing, he still likes the idea of becoming an international film star when he grows up.

TOP SECRET

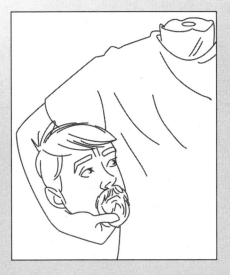

Illustrator Alan Brown's career as a freelance artist and designer has allowed him to work on a wide range of projects, from magazine illustration and game design to children's books. He's had the good fortune to work on comics such as *Ben 10* and *Bravest Warriors*. Alan lives in Newcastle with his wife, sons and dog.

OUR TOP FOUR
FEATURED TEACHERS

SPECIAL EDITION!

MR HARDY

Despite his recent retirement, Mr Hardy still tops our list. If it was wrong, he did it. If it was stupid, he said it.

Amongst the many column inches dedicated to him, who can forget his wise words when asked to explain his policy on mobile phones in school:

'The whole point of mobile phones is to keep them safely in your lockers. Even better, keep them at home where they belong.'

OUR TOP FOUR
FEATURED TEACHERS

SPECIAL EDITION!

MR JONES

He wasn't here for long, but Mr Jones comes in a close second. He may have had more brains than the rest of the teachers put together, but that still wasn't enough to stop TWW putting an end to his evil plans.

In an article wondering why he was always offering everybody sweets, TWW once described him as 'an intergalactic, purple-pigmented menace'.

And that was before we realized what he was really up to.

OUR TOP FOUR
FEATURED TEACHERS

SPECIAL EDITION!

MR CHATTERSLY

Mr Chattersly quickly found himself on the front page. It took him only three days as Acting Head Teacher to bring in the controversial ban on novelty pen tops, on the grounds of 'health and safety'. Even when he wasn't being possessed by the spirit of Victory Piggot, he still had a habit of attracting negative publicity.

When not at work, rumour has it that he likes nothing better than relaxing at home surrounded by his large collection of self-portraits.

OUR TOP FOUR
FEATURED TEACHERS

SPECIAL EDITION!

MISS BRIARS

Miss Briars may be the worst teacher in the world, but that doesn't mean she isn't up for saving it every now and again. She lives in the drama studio, but when she is let out into the open, everyone knows about it.

After last term Miss Briars became very famous on the internet. Unfortunately she still can't make it work, so she has no idea how popular she is.

HYPERSPACE HIGH

THE SCHOOL THAT'S OUT OF THIS WORLD

When John Riley catches the wrong bus, he ends up on Hyperspace High – an amazing school on a spaceship!

Light years from home, John makes friends with aliens, struggles through Galactic Geography lessons, and eats gross Martian food in the canteen.

But John needs to get up to speed fast, or he'll be booted back to Earth. Will an asteroid storm on a school trip give him a chance to prove that you don't have to be top of the class to be a hero?

READY...STEADY...RACE!

Jimmy Roberts loves watching the Robot
Races, where drivers and their super-smart
talking robots compete. When a new race for
kids is announced, Jimmy is desperate to join.
There's only one hitch – he'll never be able
to afford a robot.

But then Jimmy's grandpa reveals he's turned
his battered old taxicab into a real-life robot!

Will Jimmy and his robot Cabbie ever be able
to keep up with the competition?

OUT NOW!

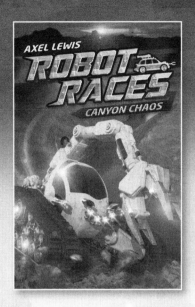

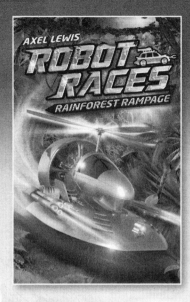

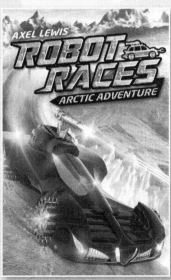

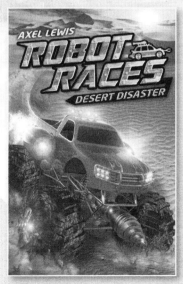

For more exciting books from
brilliant authors, follow the fox!
www.curious-fox.com